PURGATORY PRAYERS

BY

STEPHEN F. WILCOX

CB
CONTEMPORARY BOOKS
a division of NTC/Contemporary Publishing Group
Lincolnwood, Illinois USA

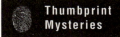

MORE THUMBPRINT MYSTERIES

by Stephen F. Wilcox:
The Hard Time Cafe
The Hidden Men

This is a work of fiction. The characters, incidents, and dialogues are products of the author's imagination and are not to be construed as real. Any resemblance to actual events or persons, living or dead, is entirely coincidental.

Cover Illustration: Adam Niklewicz

ISBN: 0-8092-0604-8

Published by Contemporary Books,
a division of NTC/Contemporary Publishing Group, Inc.,
4255 West Touhy Avenue,
Lincolnwood (Chicago), Illinois 60646-1975 U.S.A.
© 1998 Stephen F. Wilcox
All rights reserved. No part of this book may be reproduced, stored in a retrieval system, or transmitted in any form or by any means, electronic, mechanical, photocopying, recording, or otherwise, without prior permission of the publisher.
Manufactured in the United States of America.

890 QB 0987654321

Chapter 1

The tape loop at The Hard Time Cafe was playing that old Tom Jones hit, "The Green, Green Grass of Home," about a guy who's about to be executed for some crime or another.

Sergeant Harold Hafner took a moment from his sandwich to chuckle softly. He wasn't the sort to use words like *ironic*, but he had to admit it was one more thing he was starting to like about the place—that it had a sense of humor about itself.

He was a Sinatra man basically, a taste he'd picked up as a boy from hearing his old man's records. Really, any ballad would do if the singer was half-decent—Tony Bennett, Dean Martin, guys like that. Mostly the joint played old rock and country and blues stuff over the sound system, Buddy Guy, Johnny Cash, Elvis, crap that normally put his teeth on edge. But for some reason he didn't mind hearing it when he was at The Hard Time

Cafe. Because it fit the place, he supposed, like the sound of a cheesy organ at a ballgame.

"Hey, Father," Hafner said, "I got a Sinatra number you could use. How about 'That's Life'? Get it? Like a life sentence?"

Father Joe Costello swallowed a groan. "It's borderline at best, Sergeant. But I'll run it past the committee and see what they think."

The "committee" consisted of Reuben Macky, the restaurant's operations manager, and its business manager, Chet Tomzak. They were the ones who recorded the music that played throughout the restaurant each day from 11:30 in the morning until the last customers filed out sometime after nine in the evening. But anyone with a suggestion that fit the theme—it had to be about prison or some act of crime and/or punishment—could get a song added to the restaurant's playlist.

Sergeant Hafner had been trying to get some Sinatra, any Sinatra, onto the loop ever since he and his partner had started coming by for lunch on Thursday afternoons. So far, "That's Life" was as close as he'd come.

"I must say, Sergeant, you seem to be in a particularly upbeat mood today," Father Joe said.

The third man at the table, Hafner's partner, Kelvin Greene, stopped his fork midway between his salad and his mouth. "That's because we just closed a major case this morning."

"A major pain-in-the-ass case," Hafner said. "That robber-rapist that's been working the north side for a year? The one we told you about? We nabbed the little shitbird coming out of a house at five A.M."

"Well, a couple of the uniforms on patrol did."

Hafner frowned at Greene. "When I said we, I meant the special task force, okay?"

The two men weren't exactly a matched set. Hafner was married, stocky, rumpled as a pile of wash, and white; Greene was single, slim, a stylish but conservative dresser, and black. There was also a ten-year gap in their ages, with Greene the younger, and an even wider gap in their approaches to police work. Hafner was the plodder, the "just the facts, ma'am" shoe leather cop. Greene was the new breed, the thinking man's investigator, always trying to get into the perpetrator's mind.

"Congratulations in any case." Father Joe almost decided to let the subject drop, let the two men get back to their lunches, but he couldn't quite do it. "So I take it the suspect wasn't one of ours after all?"

"Nah," Hafner said, working around a large bite of his Yardbird Chicken Club. "It was some neighborhood punk with a big knife and a little—"

"Brain. A little brain," Greene cut in. He knew his partner made no distinction between talking to a fellow cop or talking to a priest. "The kid had a juvie rap sheet, is all. Mostly gang-related and vandalism charges, all when he was a minor."

"Yeah, except now he's nineteen and playing in the majors. We got his ass nailed tight for six, maybe seven robbery-rapes. In other words, Father, if you're thinking of taking him on as a new busboy, you've got about fifteen years to wait, minimum."

Father Joe studied the two sergeants. A few months earlier they had questioned three of his parolees about the case, simply because each man had a history of sexual assault. He'd protested their innocence, of course, but it hadn't cut any ice with either detective. Now he was hoping for an apology, although he knew it wasn't going to happen. The way Hafner and Greene saw it, they'd merely been doing their jobs.

And in defending his men, Father Joe reminded himself, he was merely doing his.

Father Joe Costello was pastor of Corpus Christi Catholic Church, a poor urban parish on Riverton's east side. Among the many community outreach programs his church offered was this storefront restaurant. It was staffed and operated entirely by paroled convicts, with some help from Father Joe and his assistant, Sister Matthew.

Six months earlier, the priest and his charges had realized a change was needed at the struggling restaurant. It was decided to theme the place around prisons and prisoners, in effect turning the restaurant's greatest drawback into an asset. The name was the first change—from Mercy House to The Hard Time Cafe. The interior was done over in shades of prison gray, and fake bars were painted over the windows. Menu items were renamed, like Hafner's Yardbird Chicken Club or the bowl of Jailhouse Stew Greene was enjoying with his Sing-Sing Salad.

But the most popular attraction at The Hard Time, apart from the jailhouse music on the sound system, was the ex-cons themselves. The waiters, dressed in denims and blue cotton workshirts with their names stenciled over the breast pockets, had become a floor show of sorts. The customers seemed to love asking questions and kidding with the men, and the men, Father Joe had to admit, enjoyed the attention.

"You know, I had my doubts about this place," Hafner said, echoing Father Joe's own thoughts. "But it's really turned out to be something. I'm actually getting to like it."

His partner snorted. "What you like is the price on the Thursday specials." Greene turned to the priest. "You folks have to be doing something right, Father, to get this guy in here. I swear he'd brown bag it at the Last Supper."

"Damn right." Hafner nodded. "I couldn't keep down all that kosher stuff."

Father Joe laughed. "We're happy to have your business, gentlemen. It's when you're here on business that I worry," he added pointedly.

Hafner picked up the last wedge of his club sandwich, the mayo oozing onto his fingertips. "Yeah, well, today you got nothing to worry about, Father. This is strictly lunch, right, Kel?"

"Absolutely." Greene polished off the last spoonful of stew and patted his flat belly. "And maybe supper too, considering the hour."

It was nearly half past two o'clock. Most of the lunch crowd had long since gone back to their offices and stores. The normally bustling dining room was empty except for the three men at the table and a couple of the waiters who were waiting to clear it. The rape case had kept the two detectives busy from the wee hours of the morning until after one P.M. Not that Sergeant Greene was complaining. If he had wanted regular hours, he wouldn't have joined the police force. He would've bumped up his bachelor's degree in sociology to a Ph.D. and taken a teaching job at some quiet college campus.

"Well, I'm glad you came by, as always," Father Joe said. "Now, I really should be—" He started to rise, but Hafner waved him back into the chair.

"Strictly lunch, like I said," the sergeant assured him, his eyes locked onto something at the back of the room. "But maybe you could answer just one question for me. Just an old cop's curiosity, you understand. That, uh, parolee over there. He's new, right?"

Father Joe felt a flash of anger, followed just as quickly by surrender. It was unavoidable, he knew, that policemen would always have questions about the men in the program. Once a thief, always a thief—or rapist, or murderer. That was the way of the world, according to the Harold Hafners. Suspicion had no statute of limitations.

But then, cops were professional skeptics. It's priests who were supposed to be the professional optimists. Besides, he couldn't just dismiss these particular two detectives. Some months back they had handled a case that could've been embarrassing to Corpus Christi and to Father Joe personally. The sergeants had chosen to be quiet, and he was grateful. And now he owed them his patience and trust at the very least.

Father Joe stole a glance over his shoulder. The object of Hafner's interest was a man of medium height and middle age with thinning brown hair and small, close-set eyes. "Mm, yes, that is a new man. Came aboard about two weeks ago."

"He got a name?"

Father Joe sighed. "Why do you ask, Sergeant Hafner?"

"Hey, nothing bad. I told you, it's curiosity. I got like a photographic memory for perps, is all. And somewhere, from way back, that guy looks familiar. If I don't place him, it'll drive me nuts the rest of the day."

Father Joe looked at Greene, who shrugged. "That's the way Harold is, Father. The classic one-track mind."

"I prefer 'single-minded,'" said Hafner.

"I'll bet you do."

Father Joe said, "The man's name is Frawlic, Jeffrey Frawlic."

"Frawlic. Doesn't ring any bells. What was he in for?" When he saw the priest's mouth set into a frown, Hafner added, "I can find out anyway when I get back to Metro."

"Then that's what you'll have to do." This time Father Joe did rise. "And I have things to do as well, gentlemen. I hope I'll see you again—but not until next Thursday."

* * *

"You've just always gotta piss that man off, don't you?" Greene asked.

"What'd I do? Christ, I ask one little question about one of his precious cons," Hafner complained.

They were in the squad room of the Physical Crimes Unit at Metro HQ. This was a continuation of the exchange that had taken place in their unmarked Ford on the drive back from the restaurant. An hour had passed with Greene doing paperwork alone at his desk while Hafner was off searching the law enforcement bureaucracy for information on Jeffrey Frawlic.

Now the older of the two detectives was back at his desk with a file folder in hand.

"Huh." Hafner flipped to the second yellow page and scanned it. "Mmm."

Greene couldn't help himself. "What is it?"

"Nothing." He kept reading for another half a minute. "Huh."

Greene threw up his hands. A minor in psychology and two-thirds of the way to a masters in sociology, and still he couldn't resist his partner's little teases. Even after seven years of conditioning. "All right, what? What's so damn interesting, Harold?"

Hafner looked up, his muddy brown eyes all innocent. "I thought you didn't wanna know anything. Afraid I might be violating the guy's civil rights or something, isn't that what you said?"

Greene muttered a profanity, then rose far enough to

reach across their desks and snatch the file. Hafner settled back into his gray leather-look swivel chair and folded his arms over his paunch. Humming something Sinatra-ish, to make matters worse.

After a minute, Greene looked up. "So? The guy went down for slashing his girlfriend's throat in a domestic nearly twenty years ago. Natalie Abramowitz, age nineteen at the time, worked as a cleaning woman. Apparently she was shacked up with this Frawlic. They had a fight and he killed her, a stupid, senseless murder, which could be said about all of them." He glanced at the file again. "Let's see, Frawlic was twenty-one. Part-time college student at the local JuCo and a convenience store clerk at the time. That's it, no prior record."

"Yeah. A guy with no priors. Must've been some nasty domestic. Look at the sentence."

"It's standard for Murder Two. Ten to fifteen."

"My point. The DA got Murder Two to stick with a jury on a domestic, the sort of thing gets pleaded into Manslaughter One every week. And the punk ended up doing *nineteen* years."

Greene skimmed the file again. "Okay. He picked up another few years on a conspiracy-to-commit charge, it says."

Hafner nodding. "He helped a couple other cons set up an inmate at Arcadia, standing watch while they iced the poor bastard in the showers. A real sweetheart."

"Unfortunately there's a lot of that sort of thing at Arcadia. Turf battles. So you remember the case or what?"

"Nope. But I remember the guy, I'm sure of it." He swiped a hand across his beefy face. "I just can't figure out where from—"

"After twenty years? You had to be a rookie yourself that far back."

"Second-year man. I was on patrol over in Dutchtown in those days."

"And you remember this guy from all that long ago?"

"His face, yeah. I just can't place it yet, but—"

"Oh, c'mon, man." Greene held up the yellow rap sheet. Jeffrey Frawlic's original mug shot was stapled to the upper left corner. "The guy we saw at the cafe doesn't look anything like this anymore."

"So how'd I recognize him then?"

"You *didn't*. For—" He tossed the folder back onto Hafner's littered desk. "Y'know, I can understand why that red beard of Father Joe's turns a little grayer every time he sees you coming."

"Hey, Kel? Bite me." Hafner casually stood, picked up the file, and tucked it under his arm. Then with a parting grin at his partner, he strolled across the squad room to the door, loudly humming "Luck Be a Lady."

CHAPTER 2

Billboard held up a pencil drawing of his idea and, one by one, showed it to everyone at the table. Nobody spoke for a few long seconds. Then Sister Matthew cleared her throat.

"First let me say, William, that I think the basic concept is fine. Wonderful even. Selling T-shirts with The Hard Time Cafe logo on them. Well, who'd have thought even six months ago that anyone would want them? But now, with all the interest we've seen, I definitely think it's a good idea."

"Yeah?" Billboard arched an eyebrow. "But?"

"But?" Sister Matthew fussed with a lock of her short brown hair. "Well, the problem, as I see it, is the stripes."

"Hah!" Chester Tomzak leaned forward and pointed a finger at the cafe's head chef. "I told you. People won't buy something makes 'em look like a football referee." He switched his attention to the little nun. "I told him we need to lose the black on white stripes, but he wouldn't listen to me, naturally."

"It's the prison thing, man," Billboard protested. "The stripes are cool, like Elvis in *Jailhouse Rock*."

"That was forty years ago, hillbilly," Reuben Macky said. "You probably still think a duck's-ass haircut and peach pomade are cool. These days not too many folks wanna buy a souvenir makes 'em look like a fat zebra."

"Yeah, well," Billboard said, staring darts at Macky, "a duck's ass is way cooler than a horse's ass, that's all I know. You just wish you had any kind a hair on that coconut—"

"Now, boys," Sister Matty soothed. "There's no need to get personal. This is a business meeting, and William has presented us with a business proposal. Our goal is to barnstorm and come up with the best overall—"

"I think you mean *brainstorm*, Sister," said Father Joe.

Now she gave him a look. "Whatever. The point is, William has a good marketing idea here. Let's do what we can to make it even better."

Sister Matty was the only one who called Billboard by his given name. To everyone else William Lee Ralston, former farm boy and Warlords biker, was simply Billboard. It was a nickname inspired by the colorful tattoos that adorned his arms from wrists to biceps. At the moment he had those arms crossed over his chest, the look of a man who wasn't ready to give in. But looks can be deceiving. The several years Billboard had spent in an upstate prison on drug and assault charges had taught him two valuable things: how to cook and when to back off from a fight he couldn't win.

"So we'll lose the stripes," he conceded. "But only on the T-shirts. We keep 'em on the coffee mugs."

Father Joe made a quick survey of the table, noted all the nodding heads, and made a note on his agenda.

"So be it. Stripes for the mugs, none for the T-shirts, The Hard Time Cafe logo on both. Now the question is manufacturing cost. Can we get these items made up cheaply enough to clear a profit?"

All eyes went to Chet Tomzak this time, the restaurant's business manager. Tomzak was a somewhat short and slim man with wispy dark blonde hair and a quiet manner. He'd managed a tavern in his previous life before serving four years in prison on a vehicular manslaughter conviction. That made him a natural to run the business side of the restaurant. Reuben Macky, a reformed stickup artist who had been with the program longer than any other parolee, ran the day-to-day operations—supervising the staff, seeing that supplies were ordered and delivered on time, and so on.

These five people made up the board of The Hard Time Cafe. The restaurant was closed on Mondays as well as Sundays. This was the normal Monday staff meeting, held at a table in the restaurant's dining room.

Tomzak finished running the numbers and read them back to the others. The manufacturing costs of mugs would run about three-fifty and T-shirts about nine dollars. "Meaning we could charge five bucks for the mugs and let's say twelve for the T-shirts, and we'd make a tidy profit on each. That's assuming we can move the stock, or most of it, on a month-to-month basis."

Sister Matthew and Reuben Macky had questions, which Tomzak answered. When everyone was satisfied, a vote was taken and Billboard's proposal was unanimously approved.

"Okay, next item," Father Joe said. "Sister, I understand the new man, Jeffrey Frawlic, received his driver's license the other day?"

"He did, yes, and I thought we'd act on his request to switch over part of his day from bussing the restaurant to driving the van, no pun intended."

"I wouldn't let that bastard ride in the van, let alone drive it," Reuben Macky said. "Pardon my French, Sister."

The edge in his voice, as much as the words, stopped everyone short. They all knew Macky didn't like Frawlic; he'd made that clear when Frawlic had first been introduced to the men a few weeks earlier. But no one was sure why.

Sister Matty, frowning, decided it was time to find out. "Explain yourself, Reuben. You've had it in for this man literally since day one. I know you were both at Arcadia for some of the same years, but—"

"You got that right. Same cell block—same level even—for about five years until I got my release. The little punk was in tight with the Aryan Brotherhood, all them white-power idiots."

"Hey, man," Billboard said quietly, pointing to his own forearm. There, almost hidden in the blue swirls of a professionally applied rose, were the initials AB. Like some of the others that decorated his arms, this was a jailhouse tattoo, embedded into the skin using a safety pin and burnt matchheads. But this was more than a tattoo; it was a way to show your allegiance, like wearing a Yankees cap or a T-shirt with The Hard Time Cafe logo on it.

"You know how it is in the joint, Macky. Want to or not, sooner or later you gotta mob up with one group or another. And that goes double for a skinny punk like that Frawlic. I mean, sure, I gave lip service to the Aryan Brotherhood, just like you prob'ly did with the NIC Posse or the Muslim Brothers. 'Cause you're either with 'em or agin 'em. Leastways that's how the game gets played."

Macky pulled back the sleeve of his sweatshirt, baring arms thick with cords of muscle. "You see any NIC on my arms, man? Or any Aryan Brotherhood shit on my man Tomzak here? Excuse me, Matty."

Billboard grinned. "Hell, Macky, that don't prove nothin'. You're so damn dark they'd have to use that White-Out crap for a tattoo to show up. And Chet, jeez, he wasn't in no maximum security lock-up with all these gangs and posses to worry about. I hear down there at Calderwood where he was they got dormitories, for Christ's sake—oh, is that a curse, Matty? Sorry."

Sister Matty smiled wryly. "I suppose half a loaf is better than none. If I haven't improved your salty language, gentlemen, at least I've made you aware of it."

"Oh, you've improved our language a lot, Matty. Believe me, it used to be like every other word was, uh, you know, four letters."

"Progress," said Father Joe. "Now can we get back to Reuben and his problem with Jeffrey Frawlic?"

Macky, frowning, pushed aside his empty coffee cup and tapped a Kool from the pack. He used the ritual of lighting up to think about his response. After a moment, he aimed a plume of smoke toward the high tin ceiling and started in.

"Frawlic was one of those guys you didn't really notice much, except he was always around, know what I mean? I mean, you'd be coming outa the gym or the dining hall and he'd be like *there*. Standing in a corner or against a wall by himself, doing nothing, saying nothing. Just sorta gray, blending into the place. Only, after a while, if you paid attention, you started to notice he had a way of watching everybody else. Like he was studying us. Almost like the rest of the inmates were a television show he liked to watch."

"Detached," Tomzak said, nodding. He'd noticed it about Frawlic too, but he was willing to cut the new man some slack. He'd been the new man himself not too long ago and had had his own problems fitting in. "But that could just be his expression, Reuben. It doesn't mean the guy's got his nose in the air."

"I know that, and normally I wouldn't have cared anyway. Frawlic was nothing to me. I could ignore him just as good as I ignored hundreds of other guys I saw every day. But then the little bastard joined up in the Marsden hit." He worked the cigarette again, drawing deep. "Fino Marsden was a guy I knew at Arcadia. A regular Goodtime Charlie, always had a smile, liked to joke around. You know the type. He'd give you the shirt off his back if you asked. His problem was he was a gambler, addicted to the action. It's what put him away: bunch of bad checks he put out to pay off debts. They sent him up for three-to-five on a slew of fraud charges. It doesn't take a genius to figure out what happened once he got up to Arcadia. There's always a game on up there, usually craps, but other stuff too. Fino slid by on his luck and a smile for a couple years, but then the debts he ran up in the joint caught up with him. He owed six cartons of smokes to the guy who ran the crap game, a white dude named Wardell."

He paused to grind out the stub of his cigarette. "You don't pay a loan shark on the outside, he may have somebody break your legs. You don't pay in the joint, you're history. Wardell turned Fino's debt over to his collection agency, the Aryan Brotherhood. Two of 'em went at Fino with shivs in the showers one day while our little friend Jeffrey Frawlic stood watch outside. I know because I happened to come along when it was going down, me and a couple other guys. Frawlic tried to distract us, keep us from going into the shower room, and that's when I knew what was up."

He sighed like the hiss from a deflating tire. "By the time we got inside, it was too late. Fino was dying. You could see the life going out of his eyes. They'd stuck him nine times. Me and one of the others said the hell with it and agreed to testify against Frawlic and the two who actually did the killing. They never did pin anything on Wardell, of course, but Frawlic and the other two got new time out of it. And I got pegged as a stoolie by the AB and spent my last three years at Arcadia watching my back. All because of a few boxes of cancer sticks." He leaned back in his chair. "That's what I know about the man you want to drive the church van."

The silence that followed Macky's story was broken by Sister Matty. "I've seen the man's record," she said, measuring her words, "and I won't pretend he's an angel. But then, we're not in the business of rehabilitating angels, gentlemen. And frankly, we do need a driver we can count on. You're all busy with your own work. I've got food and clothing deliveries; we have people that need to be shuttled to Social Services or the hospital. We have the hospice program to think of, and as you all know, I'm not licensed to drive myself and probably couldn't handle that brute of a van if I was."

"Well," Billboard said, "I guess we know how you'll be voting, Sister."

Macky looked at him. "How about you?"

"Me? I guess I can see two sides to it. I got no use for bushwhackers, no more than you do, man. On the other hand, I got no personal beef with the guy, and Matty does need a wheel man . . ."

Father Joe stroked his neat beard and bobbed his head minutely, as if giving himself a silent pep talk. Then he said softly, "I can't help but think of John 8:7." Everyone except Sister Matthew looked at him askance, not knowing the Biblical reference. He went on, "Jesus has just returned to the temple from the Mount of Olives and finds some of the men of the town preparing to stone a local woman, a prostitute. I'm sure you'll recognize the passage. 'He that is without sin among you, let him first cast a stone at her.'"

It was all Father Joe had to say on the subject, but it was enough. The others had too much respect for the priest and for his judgment to challenge him. When the vote was taken on whether to allow Jeffrey Frawlic to become a driver, four hands went up. Reuben Macky conceded the loss with a casual shrug of his shoulder. He wasn't going to argue any further with the man who had given him a second chance at life. But he didn't raise his hand, either.

Chapter 3

Mrs. Clooney came through the dining room's arched doorway and walked slowly across the foyer, past the open door to the church office. She nearly jumped out of her sensible shoes when she saw the intruder from the corner of her eye.

"Jay-sus!" she exclaimed. And, almost as swiftly, added, "Forgive me, Lord, for taking Thy name in vain," and crossed herself with the speed of a practiced Catholic.

"Excuse me, ma'am. I didn't mean to—"

"What're you doing here?" She recognized him now, one of Father Costello's new ones. He looked harmless, a skinny little man with thin, graying hair. But still, it pays to be careful, no matter what the Bible says about charity and forgiveness. A good dose of punishment is what most of the father's ex-convicts deserved, if you asked Margaret Mary Clooney.

Mrs. Clooney had been the housekeeper at the Corpus

Christi rectory since before Father Costello became its pastor. Almost before he'd been born. She had seen the old parish change over the years, and not for the better. She didn't understand the wisdom of bringing more criminals into a neighborhood that already had more than its share, as she'd told Father Costello more than once.

But ours is not to reason why . . .

"I asked what you're doing here. The office is closed for the noon hour. All the help is gone to lunch."

"Yes, I know. I came by to wait for Sister Matthew. To see if I'm going to be her new driver."

"Well—don't be wandering around the office then. Take a seat there and wait if you must. And don't be frightening an old woman out of her wits, popping up like that."

"Yes, ma'am, I won't."

"Hmmph." Mrs. Clooney gave him one more shot of the evil eye, then went back to her business. Provided she could remember what it was . . . Oh, yes, the throw rug in the vestibule. She'd noticed while getting the mail this morning how soiled the rug had gotten. How long had it been since she'd last had it washed? Sometime over the summer, August or possibly July.

Anyway, it was looking poorly and she intended to see that it got cleaned today while it was fresh in her mind. Ah, but it never stopped, trying to keep up with a place the size and age of this!

The rectory was really just a large old house built for the church's original pastor and his assistants. There was only one assistant pastor these days, Father Sierra, and he was shared with another parish. The first floor had a cramped kitchen, a huge dining room, and twin parlors. One of the parlors was used as the church office. There were also the large foyer and vestibule, a washroom, and a laundry area.

Father Costello's private suite, including his office, was on the second floor, as were Father Sierra's bedroom and bath, and a compact apartment for Mrs. Clooney.

Like the church itself, the house was a Gothic monstrosity. Built in the 1880s, the place was all cut red sandstone and carved gargoyles. Mrs. Clooney didn't know the first thing about architecture. What she knew about the Corpus Christi Church and rectory was that it was God's home on Riverton's east side and her home too. Regardless of its queer looks, it was a place to be cherished and guarded and kept clean in every sense of the word. Which brought her back to the soiled rug in the vestibule.

"Glory," she moaned as she bent at the waist and tried rolling it up. It seemed to get heavier with each passing month, or maybe it was just she was getting old. Well, there was no point in torturing her own back when there was a perfectly healthy man on hand.

She trundled back across the foyer to the office door. The skinny parolee was standing next to one of the desks, hands in his pockets, his gaze as vacant as a clear blue sky. Mrs. Clooney decided not to bark at him for getting up from his chair again, seeing as how she needed his help.

"You there," she said.

"Jeffrey," he said. "My name—"

"Hmmph." She curled her index finger at him, beckoning him to follow her. "I've a simple job needs doing and you strike me as just the sort for simple jobs."

"Yes, ma'am."

He followed her to the vestibule where at her command he rolled up the three-by-six rug and heaved it onto his shoulder. Then Mrs. Clooney led him down the back hall and into the laundry and mud room, which served as the back entrance into the rectory. She glanced at the washer and dryer, then thought better of it. If she put a single, heavy item like a rug into that washing machine, it would pound and shake its way across the floor as if possessed of devils. She'd have to call Mr. Arktoonian, who ran the coin-operated laundry around the corner on Braun Street, and have him send his boy around for it.

"Just take it outside and lean it against the porch railing," she told Jeffrey.

"All right." He did as he was told and returned to the utility room. When she dismissed him, however, he seemed unwilling to leave. He was looking at Mrs. Miniver, the rectory's house cat, and her new litter of kittens. They were all snuggled up in a basket tucked away beside the clothes-dryer vent.

"You're a cat fancier?" Mrs. Clooney asked, the shell around her heart softening just a bit.

"Oh, yes. I'm very fond of cats. Especially kittens."

"Well, go ahead, pick one up. Mrs. Miniver won't mind so long as you're gentle."

She watched as he went down on one knee and carefully scooped a kitten from the huddle that formed a semicircle around the mother. A black kitten with a white face and paws. He was awkward with it, holding it out away from his body. But she could see by the shine in his eyes and the half-smile on his face that Jeffrey was enjoying himself.

"We'll have to be finding them new homes soon, once they're weaned," Mrs. Clooney said. "If you're interested."

"Oh, I'd like to very much." He clutched the squirming kitten to his chest. "Only the rooming house where I'm living right now won't allow pets."

"Ah, that's too bad—"

"But I hope to be getting my own place before too long, a regular apartment. And then I'd be able to keep it. Maybe, until then, I could adopt this one and just keep it here for awhile? I could come around and feed it and take it with me sometimes when I'm doing errands in the church van."

"Well—" Mrs. Clooney hesitated. She didn't want to tell him that it would likely be a couple of years before he'd be earning enough to afford his own apartment. She'd seen other parolees try it too soon and fail. And that gaunt face of his, those faded blue eyes big as the kitten's—how could she turn away a fellow cat lover? Besides, what else did the poor man have going for him? Mrs. Clooney was a firm believer that a little feline companionship was good for the soul, maybe every bit as good as prayers and votive candles.

"I suppose it would be all right then. Provided you come around every day and take care of her. I don't mind supplying the food, but I could use help cleaning up—"

"Yes, ma'am. I'll come every day."

"See that you do. Now I—"

The back door opened before she could finish the thought. Sister Matthew, fresh from the staff meeting at the restaurant, came in, cradling in her arms a stack of papers and files. "Good afternoon, Mrs. Clooney—and Mr. Frawlic. I didn't expect to find you here."

The little nun was wearing baggy slacks and a fuzzy sweater with some kind of autumn scene knitted into it. Mrs. Clooney liked Sister Matthew very much, even if she didn't quite approve of her order's liberal dress code. It seemed to Mrs. Clooney that the world had been a better place when nuns wore habits, teachers wore suits and ties, and prayers in school were standard practice as it was back when she was a wee girl in Limerick. Less clear in her memory were the poverty and the ignorance that had prompted her to leave Ireland for the States.

"This one was waiting for you in the office," she said, "and I put him to work."

"I was hoping to hear how the meeting turned out," Jeffrey Frawlic said anxiously. "About my driving the church van, I mean."

"Yes, you've been approved by the board. You'll begin by picking up vegetables and other things for the restaurant at the Public Market tomorrow. And I may need you to drive me over to Social Services in the afternoon, and a couple of other stops."

Frawlic was grinning and nodding with such enthusiasm he forgot the squirmy kitten and almost dropped him.

"I see you've made a friend," Sister Matty said, reaching out to scratch it lightly behind the ears.

Mrs. Clooney explained the arrangement she'd agreed to, letting him claim the cat as his own but keeping it there in the rectory for now.

"That sounds like a sensible plan," the Sister said. "Have you given it a name yet, Jeffrey? Names are important, you know."

"Yes, that is so very true." Frawlic looked at her solemnly. "I'm going to sit down tonight after work and figure out the perfect name for it. Something symmetrical, I think, with no more than six letters."

"Well—" Sister Matthew sneaked a glance at Mrs. Clooney, who merely gave her a world-weary shrug. "—that's very, um, good, Jeffrey. You do that."

Chapter 4

A man, a plan, a canal, Panama. A man, a plan, a canal, Panama. A man, a plan, a canal, Panama. A man, a plan . . .

It was like a mantra for him. Or, given his surroundings, a rosary. Whenever he began to feel stress, the pressures building inside his head, he cleansed his mind by silently repeating his favorite palindrome. Yes. Cleansed. How fitting. He allowed himself a small smile as he dipped the sponge into the soapy bucket of water. Then, as he brought the sponge up and swiped it across the van's windshield, he went back to his silent chant.

A man, a plan, a canal, Panama. A man, a plan, a canal, Panama.

All right, not his favorite, perhaps. Too manufactured, too playful. His favorite palindromes were those that occurred naturally in the language but went largely unnoticed by anyone. Things that people said every day without noticing that they were spelled the same backward as forward. Names especially: Otto, Nan, Bob, Hannah. Words like *radar*. Phrases like *race car*. Now, there was a personal favorite, *race car*. R-a-c-e-c-a-r. Forward or back, same thing. It calmed him just to know that he *knew*. Unlike all the unwashed millions who walked the streets or drove past in their minivans and their Lincolns and their Toyotas, he had an understanding of the underlying meaning of the world. Of *everything*. And it continually amazed him—shocked him—how many others didn't have a clue.

It was all about letters and numbers. Numbers and letters. He had come to recognize this at an early age, perhaps nine or ten. It had been thrilling when he discovered, in the middle of his own name, Jeff Frawlic, the triple letters F-F-F. Not just the significance of a triple letter set in the middle of his name, which was hugely important in itself, three being one of the luckiest numbers of all. But those *specific* letters, F-F-F. The sixth letter of the alphabet, of course. 6-6-6. The mark of the beast.

It was good to know these things at a young age, to know what direction one's career path should take. All along, up until that tender age of nine or so, he'd thought he was the family black sheep, always finding trouble, always saying the wrong thing. His jokes weren't funny. He didn't cry at the right times or for the right reasons. He was cruel to his pets. He did not play well with other children. These were the judgments of others—his parents, the school psychologist—and he had actually believed them. That *he* was the problem. Until he'd taken those first baby steps into alpha-numerics.

Imagine his joy after finding the triple F, his lucky three, in the middle of his name, to also find his other lucky number, the number seven. Find it? It had been there in plain sight all the time. Both his first and last names, Jeffrey and Frawlic, contained seven letters each. That sort of perfection doesn't just *happen*. It is a sign for anyone smart enough to read it.

And Jeffrey Frawlic was smart enough, yes, sir. All those teen years, growing up as the black sheep. Did they think he was crying himself to sleep up there in his room? Not hardly. He'd been working out his alphanumeric system, searching for those triple-letter sets, learning the meanings behind his birth date, the letters in his hometown's name, the license plate on the family sedan. A self-educated man is what he'd become. He still fondly remembered the joy of that day when his mission became clear to him, when it fairly leaped up at him from all the numbers and the names, the words and dates that formed the center of his life on this planet.

It was all about sacrifice, wasn't it? All about young, virginal maidens giving up their purity and innocence . . .

And in prison, after the incident with Natalie—he'd handled that badly, Natalie's death, he'd admit that. It had just been bad luck for him. And, of course, bad luck for poor, stupid Natalie too. She should never have challenged him, never have threatened him, dumb bitch. She had screwed up his timetable completely.

But did he brood all those long years at Arcadia, kept from his mission? Penned in with all those hairy idiots, hardly better than apes, not one of whom had the slightest clue how the world worked? What those numbers on their shirts really meant? How the very names of their defense attorneys had a direct bearing on their fate?

No, he didn't brood. He became a better student is what he did. He read everything he could find on numbers and letters. He read about Chinese numerology. About the Indu-Arabic decimal system. About the Greeks taking their famous alphabet from the Phoenicians, who had taken their start from the Egyptians.

He learned so much that had helped him to develop his own system of alpha-numerics, but it was the little things that he most enjoyed. That the very word *alphabet* comes from the first two letters of the Greek alphabet, *alpha* and *beta*. That the Egyptians used a hieroglyph of a lotus to represent one thousand, two lotuses on a bush for two thousand, and so on. That the Mesopotamians had used not a base-ten number system, but a base-sixty system, and that a piece of that ancient system lives on today in our sixty-second minutes and sixty-minute hours.

Knowledge truly is power. After all, the devil is in the details.

Take the church van. True, he'd wanted to find a way to drive it since the day he had walked out of Arcadia and hopped the Greyhound to Riverton to begin his parole. He needed the mobility if he was to fulfill his mission. But it wasn't until he actually saw the van—the license plate, really—that he knew the vehicle would be his. That it had been chosen for him. It was so obvious to anyone who understood alpha-numerics the way Jeffrey Frawlic understood it.

He dropped the sponge in the bucket and stepped back like any working man admiring the job he'd done. It was an extended Ford Econoline van, white, with overhead air-conditioning and tinted blue windows and seating for nine. A big mother. But he wasn't really looking at the van or admiring his wash job. He was staring lovingly at the front license plate: 4D7 J3F.

Well, the meaning of 4D7 was crystal clear: Sacrifice number four, a girl with D for her initials, would prove to be lucky (the 7) for him. But the rest of the license number was equally revealing to anyone who bothered to really look at it. Not only did it contain his initials, J-F, but the *combination* of J3F told him the exact day and hour when he would resume his special work. J, of course, was the tenth letter of the alphabet, representing the tenth of September, which was his release date from Arcadia. The 3 meant he was to resume his special work in three-times-ten days from his release date, or thirty days. And the F, naturally, meant six o'clock. Simple.

At six o'clock on October 10, some nine days from now, he would accomplish his fourth sacrifice. For that, too, was ordained. Because October 10 was also the twentieth anniversary of his third sacrifice . . .

"Hey!"

Jeffrey Frawlic blinked once, the small satisfied smile melting away into his normal blank expression. Only then did he turn toward the person who had called to him. It was Reuben Macky, as he had feared. That big jig had it in for him, and he wished he knew how significant the threat was. After all, the bastard had already cost him five extra years in jail; he was an enemy to be reckoned with. Still, Jeffrey had tried evaluating Macky's name, the letters and their corresponding numbers, to see if there was any special meaning or power contained in them, but nothing had come of it. By alpha-numeric reasoning, Macky had no role in Jeffrey's fate. That was good, of course. It was always better to control one's own destiny, and knowing Macky posed no real threat was—reassuring. But he still wished the big black brute would leave him alone.

He put on a friendly grin. "Morning. It looks like a beautiful fall day ahead."

"Yeah. Too bad we've all got work to do." Macky kicked at the bucket, sending a soapy wave splashing over the rim. "You gonna use up most of it sudsing this van, the way you're going."

"Oh. I guess I was daydreaming. I've been out three weeks as of today, and I'm still trying to get used to the idea of it, being a free man. I'm sure you know what I mean."

Macky didn't want to admit having anything in common with Frawlic, not even that odd floating sensation he remembered so well during the first few weeks of his own release from prison. So he said, "I don't know what you mean and I don't care what you mean. I want you to hose off and wipe down this van before you get soap spots all over it. Then I want you to get your ass back into the restaurant and help Spinelli and Donzell set up for the lunch crowd."

"But, you see, I'm driving the nun and some boxes of old clothes to people's houses today and—"

"The *nun* has a name, asshole. And you ain't driving Sister Matty anyplace until one o'clock, which means you got plenty of time to help us set up for lunch." Macky felt like popping him, just one time, punch a hole in his face to replace that sick little grin. Just once. Instead, he jabbed a stiff finger at him. "I catch you slacking off and I'll get Father Joe to pull your van privileges in a heartbeat. Then I'll have you inside peeling spuds until you don't ever wanna see another potato so long as you live. We understand each other?"

Jeffrey nodded meekly. That was the last thing he wanted, to lose this van. He was never good at making friends, but he decided he needed to try with Macky, if only to keep him off his back. "You know, uh, Reuben," he said. "You probably don't realize how lucky we all are to be placed here at Corpus Christi."

"I've been in the program six years, man. Don't tell me I don't know how good Father Joe's been to me."

"No, I don't mean the priest. Not the people or anything like that." He hoped the exasperation he felt at the man's ignorance wasn't betrayed by his voice. Talking to people of this sort was never easy for him, but he'd been trying to learn patience. "I mean the name, Corpus Christi Catholic Church. You see?"

But it was obvious he didn't. Macky stared back at him with those big dumb brown eyes of his, as if he were some disgusting crawly thing in a petri dish. Jeffrey, fighting to remain calm, exhaled. "It's plain as the nose on your face, Macky. Corpus Christi Catholic Church? C-C-C-C?"

"What the hell are you babbling about?"

"You don't see it?" He couldn't help himself; he laughed scornfully. "Lookit, what's your lucky number?"

"Lucky number? Jesus," Macky muttered. "My lucky number is two, which is how many seconds you got to pick up that hose and finish up on this van, okay?"

Jeffrey shook his head. Try and be nice to some people. "C is the *third* number of the alphabet. Three is one of the luckiest of all numbers, and we've got a *quad* set going for us here. C-C-C-C. I mean, I can't believe anyone can be so stupid they can't understand—"

Macky reached out and snatched him by the front of his shirt, dragging the much smaller man up onto the tips of his tennis-shoed toes. "Let me tell you what's stupid, numbnuts. Calling a guy names who outweighs you by a hundred pounds, that's stupid. Trying the patience of your supervisor, that's stupid. And annoying the hell out of a guy who already hates your guts, that's really stupid. But you know what's stupidest of all, Frawlic? Believing in a bunch of goddamn magic numbers—now that is truly freakin' stupid!"

* * *

"You shouldn't let him get to you," Chet Tomzak said. He was on a stool pulled up to the kitchen's big stainless steel prep table, wolfing down a ham and Swiss before the doors opened for the lunch crowd.

Macky merely grunted at first. He had just come in from the alley. Through the window in the kitchen door, both men could see Frawlic hosing off the church van.

Meanwhile, all around them, Billboard and his kitchen crew hustled, turning heads of lettuce and pecks of tomatoes and peppers into tossed salad, firing up the grill, mixing the batter for biscuits, and dumping bags of frozen french fries into the fryer.

"You saw it, huh?" Macky said, grabbing a stool.

"Yeah, and you're lucky Father Joe didn't. Getting physical with the little creep, that's really not a good idea, Reuben."

"All I did was wrinkle his shirt! And told him to quit screwing around and get his butt inside to help set up. Jesus, his first day as a driver and he thinks he owns that van."

"I'm just saying," Tomzak said, "you know how Joe feels about giving guys space, especially when they're new to the program."

"Ah, hell, I know that. It's just—I don't know—Frawlic pisses me off is all."

Billboard slipped past him, lugging a beef roast fresh from one of the restaurant's three ovens. "Jesus, get over it, man," he said, setting the roasting pan down at one end of the table. "So the guy helped set up one of your friends in the joint. We've had a lotta worse bad-asses come through here. This clown offed his girlfriend for who knows why—that ain't even a blip on the radar screen."

"Yeah, well, maybe so, but at least most of 'em came into the program looking for a fresh start. This guy Frawlic, I don't know. I got the distinct feeling he's just going through the motions, gonna slide by until it suits him, then take off on us. And it won't surprise me one bit if he steals the van in the bargain."

"I hope you're wrong," Tomzak said. "But even if you're not, you know Joe's motto. 'Every man starts with a clean slate.'"

"Yeah, yeah."

"Whatever," Billboard said. He carved a slice from the end of the roast, the meat pink inside with the juices running clear, and held it out to Macky on a fork. "Here, big guy, try this for flavor."

Macky put the whole piece in his mouth and chewed slowly. "Mmm-m-m."

"It's okay?"

"Well, it's hard to say, a piece that small. Might take a few more slices, along with some wheat bread and a smear of horseradish, before I could say for sure."

Billboard looked over at Tomzak, a wry frown creasing his angular face. "See, man? That's how you chill out a pissed-off pit bull. You give him some old-fashioned, all-American red meat to chew on."

"With horseradish," Macky reminded him.

CHAPTER 5

The following Thursday, Hafner and Greene made their regular lunch visit to The Hard Time Cafe, arriving a few minutes past one o'clock. The loop was playing an oldie from the Fifties, "Riot in Cell Block Number 9" by The Robins. The noon crowd was lingering over its coffees and the ever popular Cheese-It-The-Cops cheesecake slices, so the two cops had to wait briefly for a table. While they waited in front by the cashier's counter, Greene swayed to the music and Hafner scanned the faces.

"Hey!" he said. "I know that guy."

"Oh, no, not this again," Greene said. "Harold, the place is full of ex-cons, okay? Get used to it."

"No, not a con. Over there at that table there, see? The old guy sitting with the good-looking black babe."

That last part was enough to catch Greene's undivided attention. He found the table and, after several seconds of checking out the woman, reluctantly sized up her companion. They seemed an unlikely pair, a pretty young black woman in a brown silk pantsuit and a gray-haired, grizzled-looking white guy in a checked short-sleeve shirt.

"That's my old rabbi from when I first joined the force," Hafner said. "My mentor, as they say these days. Tony Spola. Jeez, I wonder what he's up to."

"Let's find out," Greene said. "It's a table for four."

They made their way over, weaving through the crowded dining room. Greene stood by patiently while Hafner and the old man exchanged greetings and handshakes, content to nod and smile at the young woman and wait for an introduction.

"Oh, Tony, this here is my partner, Kelvin Greene. We work out of the Physical Crimes Unit down at Metro. Kel, this is Tony Spola, one of the best old-time homicide dicks this town ever had."

"Old-time!" the retired cop protested, smiling as he and Greene shook hands. "You better watch it, Haffy. One of these days they'll push you out the door too, and you'll wonder where all the years went."

Greene looked at Hafner. "Haffy?"

"Old nickname. Forget it," he muttered. "And who do we have here, Tone? You back in circulation with the ladies?"

Spola laughed. "I would, but my wife'd kill me. No, this young lady is with the newspaper, a reporter. Miss L. J. Trudeau. She's been bugging me, wanting to interview me about an old case. So I figured I'd get her paper to spring for a free lunch out of the deal."

The introductions went around again with Greene holding onto the reporter's hand a couple seconds longer than necessary. She didn't seem to mind, though.

"We figured we'd invite ourselves to join you," Hafner

said. "If that won't cramp your style, Miss Trudeau."

"Normally I like to do interviews one-on-one, but I guess a couple more Metro detectives can't hurt. I'll be interested in your takes on the story," she said, looking mostly at Greene. "And my name's Lena. I use L. J. Trudeau just for my byline."

The men took chairs on either side of her. She was even better looking up close, Greene thought, taking in the big hazel eyes, the dazzling smile, the smooth milk-chocolate skin. Now if the legs were as long as they appeared to be, tucked away under the table . . .

"The alphabet murders?" His partner's voice brought Greene's attention back to what Lena Trudeau was saying. "Why all of a sudden are you interested in that old case?" Hafner said.

"For the obvious reasons, Sergeant. It's the most famous set of unsolved murders in this city's history. It involves a serial killer who got away. And next Wednesday marks the twentieth anniversary of the last murder."

Hafner wasn't buying. "Jesus. We haven't got enough current crime, you gotta dredge up that old tragedy?"

"Exactly what I tried to tell her, Haffy," Spola said, "but you can't argue with the media. A story's a story, right, Miss Trudeau?"

Hafner watched Spola take a pack of Camels from his shirt pocket and shake out a cigarette. He almost said something. The old man had been pushed into retirement because of a bad ticker, as Hafner recalled. But he told himself it wasn't his place to be telling a seventy-year-old how to live.

Spola looked older than the last time Hafner had seen him a few years back at somebody else's retirement party. Naturally he was a little grayer these days. Certainly thicker of body and thinner of hair than he had been twenty years ago. Back when Sergeant Tony Spola had been the veteran city police detective and Harold Hafner had been an eager young patrolman. Back in the days when the alphabet killings were front-page news, big enough to push the doings in Iran below the fold in the morning newspaper.

Spola let out a plume of smoke with a sigh. "The so-called alphabet murders were a nightmare. A nightmare, young lady, and—it pains me to say it—the Riverton PD's worst failure. It's the kind of case that stays with a cop like a bad smell that soaks into your clothes and you can't never get rid of it. That stink of failure is always there to remind you."

Hafner grunted his agreement. Greene, who only knew of the case from half-forgotten headlines and bits he'd picked up around the squad room over the years, sat back, eager to listen.

Lena Trudeau was too young to have any memory of the awful murders of three little girls. But the clips files back at her newspaper had told enough to show the horror of the crimes. How each of the victims had probably been grabbed off the street on their way home from school, strangled, and sexually molested, and their bodies dumped in vacant lots.

And yet she was still surprised by the heat in the old man's words after all these years. She listened closely as, alternating between sips of coffee and deep drags on the cigarette, he told of his role in the investigation.

"Me and my partner didn't catch the first case, Anna Andrechuk. But when the second little girl was found six months later—"

"Brenda Bragos?" The reporter had her notepad open on the table, her pen ready in her hand.

"Yeah. We were assigned to the team for the Bragos girl, and by the time the third one turned up dead six months after that—that would be Catherine Cazminski—just about everybody in the department was in on the investigation. A task force, they called it. More like the Air Force, all the hotshots they had running around.

"But to no avail. The case was never solved. The victims were three little girls, two of them ten and the other eleven years old, each with double initials. Murdered in alphabetical order approximately six months apart.

"A-B-C straight through for the names of the victims. The papers also called it the double-initial murders at first, but the name that stuck was the alphabet murders.

"Each of the girls came from roughly the same city neighborhood, known since the nineteenth century as Dutchtown but long since populated with a mix of central and eastern European immigrants and southern black families. Each was the product of a troubled home, no father in the house, mother on some form of assistance. Meaning that each girl's family had been involved in some way with the county's Department of Social Services.

"We figured the killer had to have some kinda connection to either the neighborhood schools or Social Services to be able to choose and stalk the victims the way he did. And we know he used a kitten to lure the girls into his car, because the technicians found white cat hairs as part of the fiber evidence on each of the bodies."

"Right," Hafner spoke up. "The cat hairs. That was one of the details the task force held back from the press at the time, wasn't it, Tone?"

"Yeah, to help sort out all the sickos who were coming in, trying to take credit. Can you imagine?" He shook his head. "In church whenever the priest gives a sermon on good and evil, I think of that bastard and his kitty, stalking those poor children."

"I understand what evidence you had is largely

destroyed or missing now," said Lena Trudeau.

"Yeah, well," Spola waved his hands, "they'd never make a case on what little we had anyway. There was virtually no physical evidence left behind by the killer. What we mostly had to work with was from looking at opportunity and past records and the like. We questioned a hell of a lot of suspects just because they worked for the county DSS and some of their co-workers thought they were a little weird."

Hafner had something nagging at the back of his brain. But before he could bring it forward, his partner interjected himself into the conversation with a typical college-boy question. "Did you have a professional profile done on the killer?" Greene asked Tony Spola. Trying to impress the babe, Hafner figured.

"We had the department's shrink work with a specialist from the FBI," Spola said. "What they came up with wasn't exactly a news flash. Basically, it confirmed we were looking for a young male loner, a social misfit who probably worked a menial job and had few friends. The usual stuff except for the part about his obsession with double initials and alphabetical order. That wasn't standard, but it didn't really tell us anything we didn't already know, either."

Then Trudeau asked one of those reporter's questions intended to produce a good quote for high up in the story, the second or third paragraph, possibly even the lead.

"What I remember most about the case?" The retired detective's furry eyebrows rose then fell as his eyes pinched shut in recall. "The sight of the Bargos girl lying all—ruined, out there in that field. Both her little hands clutching bits of dirt and weeds like a testament to how much she struggled to get away. To save herself."

In the moments that followed, Spola silently smoked and the two younger men ordered their lunches. Lena Trudeau scribbled words into the notepad, adding a few descriptive adjectives to describe the old cop's demeanor: *strained . . . angry . . . still pained by the memories after so long.*

Presently she said, "You must wonder why the killer stopped after three murders. I mean, you must've theorized over the years. Did he move out of the area? Did he maybe die suddenly, or get sent off to jail for some unrelated crime?"

"Well," Spola stared into his coffee mug, "I wouldn't know the answer to that, so I guess I can't comment."

"Ignorance of the outcome didn't stop some of your former colleagues from commenting. Mike Merrill had plenty of theories about the case," she said.

"That old windbag. Ignorance never stopped him from doin' nothin'. He wasn't even one of the lead investigators, just did a lot of follow-up interviews." He sipped at the coffee. "It's what I was sayin', there's really nobody much left anymore who was on the inside of the investigation. Just me and Lou Carragio—Lou and his partner, Sam Jeffries, were the primaries. Jeffries dropped dead years ago while he was still on the job, and I hear Lou's as good as gone himself."

Trudeau nodded. "He's in a nursing home in the city. I tried to interview him, but—well, he's in the advanced stages of Alzheimer's."

"God's mercy on him," Spola said reflexively. "I don't know what it is. All the stress, I guess. The average life span for cops has to be ten, twelve years shorter than for the average guy."

"Seems that way," Hafner agreed. "I was at a funeral just last month for a guy, took early retirement and opened up a little woodworking business. Six years later he drops dead with some kind of stroke. Fifty-one years old. You might've known him, Tony—Mick Flatley?

Worked out of Traffic Control a lotta years."

"Didn't know him. Y'know, my old partner, Ben Garfield, went eleven years ago. Cancer." A small, wistful smile softened Spola's heavily lined face. "We used to kid about death when we were younger, me and Ben. He'd say if he died first I should sit shivah for seven days, I could do the rosary for him. And I'd tell him, 'Hey, if I go first you'll have to pull a novena, nine days. Maybe sing me one of those songs for the dead like that guy who sings in your temple.' And Ben'd say, 'Ya mean the cantor?' And me—" A guttural laugh. "—I'd say, 'Yeah, Eddie Cantor. Sing me a tune like Eddie Cantor.' We'd kid back and forth like that, Ben and me."

The others chuckled politely at the story. Tony Spola seemed lost in memories for a moment. Then he said, "Another thing we used to talk about was how we'd never be able to find any peace until we got the sick bastard who did those murders. All the guys on the investigative team said it. And I believe it still today that Ben, Lou Carragio, all of 'em, even the victims—especially the victims—won't be at peace until justice is done for those little girls."

He looked squarely at Lena Trudeau. "I guess a kid like you might think that's an old-fashioned idea, justice. Like the Golden Rule and the Latin Mass and a lotta other things we used to believe in in my day. Well, young lady, I still believe in 'em."

CHAPTER 6

He couldn't get the song out of his head.

"Someone's in the kitchen with Dinah, someone's in the kitchen I know-oh-oh-oh. Someone's in the kitchen with Di-NAH, strummin' on the old banjo . . ."

He sang it under his breath and hummed the parts where he wasn't sure of the words. It was starting to bug him, the way the tune had crept into his brain and taken over. It wouldn't let him concentrate on his alphanumeric combinations, and that wouldn't do. He needed the numbers and letters coursing through him the way a junkie needs methadone in his veins—to keep him steady.

"Someone's in the kitchen with—*Stop*!" he ordered himself as he slammed on the brakes for a light that had turned yellow.

"Jesus, Frawlic! What up with you, man?" Donzell Jessup was in the back of the church van, steadying cartons of eggs stacked atop a crate of iceberg lettuce. Jeffrey Frawlic was behind the wheel, driving west along Carson Avenue. It was a sunny Tuesday morning, and they were returning from a pickup at the Riverton Public Market.

Jessup was a waiter at The Hard Time Cafe. Now in his thirties, he had wasted much of his youth breaking into houses and Mom-and-Pop stores to feed a crack habit. It had cost him two stretches in the joint, the last one a six-year gig that had ended just twelve months ago when he'd been paroled into Father Joe's program.

So Donzell Jessup knew all about uncontrollable urges. But he didn't know about Frawlic's particular thing with the numbers and shit. All he saw was a pasty white dude humming something, always with this dumbass little grin. Man, Donzell did not care for that little grin, but he wasn't gonna rock no boats. Macky may have some serious issues with the little mother, but Donzell wasn't interested. Another eighteen months of parole, he'd be free and clear, get hisself a job up at one a those midtown restaurants where the tips are good for like three, four hundred a week.

Still, he had responsibilities to think about. They got back with a bunch of busted eggs or banged-up produce, and Billboard would carve the both of them a new asshole. So he said, "You high or somethin', man, standin' on the brakes like that for a lousy yellow light?"

Frawlic's hollow blue eyes stared back at him from the rearview mirror. "I wouldn't want a ticket my first week with a new license."

"Let me clue you in, man. They got three colors on them lights; red means stop, green means go, and yellow means go *faster*, okay? I mean, you be stoppin' sudden like that, the cars behind us gonna run right up your tailpipe. Then we be *wearin'* all these eggs and shit."

"Point taken," Frawlic said.

Jessup rolled his eyes.

* * *

She was perfect. Dinah DiMaria, age eleven, a bit small for her age. A fifth-grade student at Holy Sacrament School, an elementary school that Corpus Christi co-sponsored along with a couple of other city parishes. He'd found the name in the records kept at the church office, the children's section; files full of names and birth dates and home addresses. Which schools they attended, whether they took religious instruction, or had taken First Communion, or belonged to the CYO or any after-school programs.

He'd almost missed it that day when that busybody housekeeper had found him hanging around the office during lunch hour. He heard her footsteps approaching from the foyer and was about to close the files when the name all but leaped out at him: Dinah DiMaria—double Ds. Not only that, but the girl lived over in Dutchtown on the city's northeast side, Frawlic's old stomping grounds. Triple Ds!

Perfection.

And he'd been so worried after all these years that destiny would've deserted him, perhaps moved on to someone younger. He'd worried that he'd be unable to find sacrifices without Natalie's help. Not that Natalie had known she was helping him; not at first, anyway.

Poor stupid Natalie. Imagine being a cleaning woman at nineteen and knowing, in those private moments when you allow yourself the truth, that you'll never be anything more than you are. It was pitiful really. She was, to be honest, better off dead. If only it hadn't created such a mess for Jeffrey . . .

He'd met her at the community college one night in the late 1970s after a late class. Natalie was on the cleaning crew, taking a break in the big lounge at the student union. He'd bought her a soft drink, sat, and chatted with her awhile. He remembered the annoying disco music that was playing in the background. And he remembered how he had talked on and on about alpha-numerics. How everything in life was controlled by the seemingly random letter and number combinations that were all around us. She didn't understand, of course, but she listened. That was the thing; she really listened to him.

Things came together in a hurry after that. They dated a few times, then Natalie moved in with him in his one-bedroom apartment on Parsells Place. He learned early on about her other job, one night a week cleaning offices over at the county complex including the Department of Social Services. He had seen the possibilities immediately. All those years of studying numbers and letters had finally come together. Natalie was to become his stalking horse.

Until she finally figured out what he'd been doing, seeing the newspaper stories about the little girls, the double initial stuff. Knowing he'd been questioned by the cops. She went haywire, stupid cow, and he'd been forced to shut her up. Unfortunate, because up to then everything had worked so well.

It had been so simple, that was the beauty of it. He'd meet Natalie at the Social Services offices for a late-night snack every now and again, a romantic gesture on his part. Or so Natalie thought. Then he'd rifle through the files while she was off in the ladies' room . . .

Anna Andrechuk.

A shudder of pleasure went down his spine as he thought of his first sacrifice, plucked from the AFDC files like a delicate flower growing in a garbage heap. If only she had understood the honor he was doing her, she wouldn't have struggled so. None of them would.

Brrr-innnggg.

The bleat of the school bell brought Jeffrey Frawlic

back to the present. It was 3:10 on a gentle October day. He was sitting in the church van, parked in a lot at a convenience store on the corner of Elmar and Lowell Avenue. Across the street, surrounded by a chain-link fence, was Holy Sacrament Catholic Elementary School, and that bell signaled the end of the school day.

"Oh, yes."

He felt another shudder as he watched the children begin to file out. Most went to the orange buses that lined the driveway circle in front of the school. But some, alone and in groups of two and three, spilled out onto the sidewalks on Lowell Avenue and the side street, Elmar. From there they walked home, or to an after-school program, or to the local hangout for Cokes and candy. In a few cases a parent was waiting outside the fence, ready to walk the child home safely.

Frawlic was surprised to see almost as many fathers as mothers. Times have changed in twenty years, he thought.

He spied her exiting onto Elmar Street and turning right, north. Yes, that was correct. Home was in that direction and this being Tuesday rather than a Monday or a Thursday, little Dinah DiMaria would be going straight home instead of to her piano lesson. Straight home to an empty house since Dinah was a latchkey child, her divorced mother not due home from her job until four-thirty.

Frawlic reviewed these facts as he pulled the van from the lot and, instead of pulling out to the left to follow her down Elmar, he went right onto Lowell Avenue. This was the third time in a week he had observed his young sacrifice. What he hadn't found out from the church records, he had gleaned from watching Dinah, her house, her mother's arrival times. He'd even called the house once at four o'clock, asking for the mother, Angela, who of course wasn't there. Little Dinah, that sweet precise voice of hers thrilling him, saying, "She can't come to the phone right now. Can I take a message?"

Two blocks down Lowell he turned left onto Waverly. He followed it for about a quarter mile, past the small green rectangle called Washington Park. At Crossman Street he hung another left, continuing for a short block and then pulling to the curb.

It was a street of small bungalows with tiny yards and narrow driveways leading to single-car garages in back. Some were neat and well cared for while others looked as shabby and neglected as their owners. Number 73—a perfect number—fell somewhere in between. The lawn was a bit ragged and the strip of shrubs along the front was overgrown, but the house itself was presentable enough.

Jeffrey Frawlic stared at it through the van's tinted windshield. He thought about his own upbringing in a house not too different from this one on a street not too far from here. He thought about the aloneness he'd felt growing up there, confined in that small house with his brain-dead family . . .

And then there she was again! Little Dinah DiMaria coming up the sidewalk from the other direction. She was all by herself, wearing her violet backpack and swinging her arms.

He watched as she turned in at number 73 and dug the key from her pocket and let herself in. Yes. So far, so good. Three days, same result. Lucky three. And tomorrow, no more dry runs.

Tomorrow was for real. His destiny—and hers—awaited.

Frawlic restarted the church van and slowly pulled away from the curb, happily singing, "Someone's in the kitchen with Dinah, someone's in the kitchen I know-oh-oh-oh . . ."

Chapter 7

Reuben Macky couldn't leave it alone.

It ate at him, seeing Jeffrey Frawlic every day. That superior smile always at the corners of his mouth, the wide eyes constantly watching others when they weren't paying attention. But Macky was paying attention. He had seen that look on Frawlic's face before, outside the D-Block showers at Arcadia—a look of calm indifference. Show him a bug getting squashed or a baby choking, it would be the same to Jeffrey Frawlic, just something to watch.

Like we're all some freakin' television show put on to amuse him, Macky thought. The man was stone cold, like Death in denims and tennis shoes. And getting away with murder around here. It was just too damn much.

Tuesday had been bad enough. For the third time in a week, Frawlic had gone off to do errands and deliveries with the church van, only to disappear for an extra hour or two. Macky had complained to Sister Matty about it, but she had dismissed it. "He's probably just out driving around, enjoying his freedom."

Fine. Macky didn't like it, but he told himself that if nobody else cared that the little weasel was goofing off, not pulling his weight, so be it. But then he arrives at the restaurant that morning, Wednesday, and what does he find? While Ernie and Billboard and Donzell and everybody else is scurrying around, scrambling to get the restaurant up and running in time for its 11:30 opening, Frawlic is sitting in the back door of the van, the liftgate up, his feet dangling out over the bumper, reading a goddamn newspaper.

"All right, numbnuts, that's it." Macky walked up and kicked Frawlic's foot. "Get your worthless butt inside and start doing your job. Which, if I got anything to say about it, ain't gonna include driving this van anymore."

Frawlic lowered the newspaper and leveled his washed-out blue eyes at the other man. "Fortunately, you don't have anything to say about it." And resumed reading his paper.

Normally Frawlic or any of the ex-cons would jump when Reuben Macky got on their case. But Frawlic was feeling cocky. After all, it was the day he'd been planning for two decades now, and all the signs were positive. Even the newspaper he was reading confirmed the importance of this day, the twentieth anniversary of his last sacrifice. If only the reporter hadn't used so many negative words to describe his actions—barbarous, cruel, predatory.

But she couldn't be expected to understand the big picture. None of them could. Certainly not this great black ape standing in front of him.

Macky couldn't believe it. The little son of a bitch was ignoring him. He snatched the paper away.

"Hey, give me that—"

"When I tell you to move, punk, I expect you to *move*." He tossed the crumpled newspaper onto the ground.

"You ignorant nigger bastard," Frawlic hissed, as he uncoiled himself from the van.

All the safety valves Reuben Macky had learned in his years in prison and his years since were forgotten. In that one moment of rage, all he could see was the pinched face of a bigot, and all he could hear was the racial slur that had been hurled at him.

With a howl, he grabbed Frawlic's shirt with his huge left hand. With his right he began throwing punches: a straight shot to the eye, an uppercut to the jaw, a finishing punch to the gut that literally took the little man's breath away. Then, with no more effort than he'd used to toss aside the newspaper, Macky hurled Frawlic halfway across the alley. He banged against the dumpster and dropped to the ground in a heap.

"Jesus, Macky." Billboard came out from the kitchen, along with some of the other men. They'd been watching from the windows. "You tryin' to get your ticket pulled, man? 'Cause, you ask me, I don't think this here little redneck's worth it."

"Piss on him."

"Looks like you already did."

Sister Matty elbowed her way through the half-circle of men blocking the door from the kitchen. "What is it? What's happened?" When she saw Frawlic, just then trying to pick himself up, her hand went to her mouth. "Dear Lord, Jeffrey, are you all right? My goodness, what is this all about?" she asked, her eyes lasering in on Macky.

"I'll tell you what it's about," he bellowed. "Am I the operations manager of this restaurant or not? And is this punk part of my wait staff or not? Because I'll be damned if I'm gonna put up with one minute more of his crap."

Matty had heard Macky holler before, but never quite so loud and never at her. And she didn't care for it one little bit. She screwed her face into a frown and stepped right up to him, nose to chest.

"Stop your yelling," she said. "Of course, you're the operations manager, but that doesn't give you the right to beat up your employees."

"I've got a right to expect some work out of them, don't I? And a right not to have to listen to any smart-mouth trash talk—"

"You cannot *hit* people, Reuben, no matter the provocation, short of self-defense. You know that!"

Macky, seething, walked away, then came back to her and stuck out a finger for emphasis. "I know this! That piece of white-is-right, honky mother-lovin', blue-eyed shit-for-brains is *not* workin' in my restaurant no more! You want a driver? You got one, full time. Just keep him the hell away from me before I kill the son of a bitch."

* * *

"Jesus, Mary, and Joseph! Whatever happened to you?"

Mrs. Clooney began clucking, going into her mother-hen mode, even reaching out to touch the bruises on Jeffrey Frawlic's face. He shrank away from her. The skin must still be tender, she thought.

They were in the back entry of the rectory, the mud room. Mrs. Clooney had just brought a tray up to Father Costello in his second-floor office and was thinking of having a bite of lunch herself when she'd heard the doorbell ring.

"It's that Macky," Frawlic told her, his eyes cast down at the linoleum floor. "He hates me from when we were in prison together. Because I wouldn't do—things for him and his friends. Disgusting things. He's been telling people lies about me and threatening me ever since."

Mrs. Clooney clucked some more. "You poor man." She could only imagine the terrible and vile things that went on in those prisons. "Sit yourself down and tell me all about it, why don't you?"

"I can't, ma'am. The Sister wants me to drive one of the parishioners to the hospital for an appointment. Then I have to swing around to an address she gave me and pick up some boxes of stuff for the used clothing shop. I came by to see if it'd be okay if I took Fluffy along for the afternoon. It's such a nice day and all."

"So, you've given our little kitty a name. Fluffy—it suits him."

Frawlic nodded. "It's perfect, numbers-wise."

* * *

And it was. He'd spent a lot of time on it, bouncing names around, writing them in his notebooks, studying them for their numerical power. He'd rejected dozens of possibilities, everything from Frodo to Sylvester, before hitting on Fluffy.

F-L-U-F-F-Y, translated to corresponding numbers, equaled 6-12-21-6-6-25. Now, the significance of the three sixes was obvious. But then you add the 1 and 2 of the twelve, which makes a 3, and add the 2 and the 1 of 21, which makes 3 again, and add the 2 and the 5 in 25, which was 7, and you had 6-3-3-6-6-7. It was undeniably good luck! Triple sixes, double threes, and his personal number, seven.

These were the numbers and combinations that nearly constantly ran through his head—threes, sixes, and sevens, representing luck, destiny, and personal achievement. Oh, and there was one other, the number nine, which, as everyone knew, was the square of three and which represented completion. Before he was finished, he would sacrifice nine perfect virgins, following strict alphabetical order. And then his mission would be complete. *He* would be complete, truly complete, for the first time in his life. Because the ninth letter of the alphabet was *I*.

As in *I, Jeffrey Frawlic* . . .

But he was getting ahead of himself. There was the little matter of sacrifice number four, his sweet double-D from Dutchtown, to deal with.

It was a quarter past three in the afternoon and cloudy—the blue sky above having gone gray and threatening. The church van once again cruised down Crossman Street but from the other direction today, pulling to the curb almost in front of number 73.

"Someone's in the kitchen with Dinah, someone's in the kitchen I know-oh-oh-oh."

Frawlic looked himself over in the van's rearview mirror, taking in the black eye and the yellowing bruise on the side of his chin. He didn't have to look to remember the punch to his stomach; he could feel it every time he breathed. Still, nothing broken—that, surely, was one more sign of good luck. In fact, Macky may've done him a favor, working him over like that. It would make him more believable.

He took from his shirt pocket the sunglasses he'd picked up at a convenience store and put them on. That helped hide the ugly mouse under the eye and also hid the eyes themselves. That was important. He'd learned early on that people didn't trust his eyes. He didn't understand why, but he didn't fight it, either. He always wore dark glasses when harvesting a sacrifice.

He checked the mirror again with the glasses, satisfied with the look. Then he reached over to the passenger seat and grabbed the crutch. He had lifted it from outside a room at St. Mary's earlier that afternoon while he was there dropping off that disgusting old Italian lady who wouldn't shut up about her cholesterol count.

"Someone's in the kitchen with Di-NAH, strummin' on the old banjo."

He turned and looked over his shoulder. The kitten was up on one of the seats, playfully slapping at a piece of donated clothing that hung over the side of a cardboard box. Through the back door's window he could see to the corner of Crossman and Elmar. Any moment now, little Dinah DiMaria would be coming around that corner. Any moment . . .

There she was!

He fumbled with the door handle, then forced himself to stop and take a deep breath. Okay. Now take your time, execute the plan. Stay—with—the—plan.

He slowly got out of the van and, leaning heavily on the crutch, hobbled around to the sidewalk. He slid open the van's side door and gingerly lowered himself down to a sitting position in the door, laying the crutch on the pavement.

"C'mere, Fluffy," he cooed. "C'mon."

All right, he had the cat in hand. Now when the girl got close, he'd let the animal jump down to the sidewalk and scoot around. Then he'd stumble getting up and ask the girl to please help catch his kitty for him. When she caught it and brought it back to the open door of the van, he'd shove her inside and after that, for the next few hours until six—

"Not this time, Frawlic."

He jerked around at the unexpected voice.

"No, no, no," he whined. "Not you again!"

Chapter 8

Tom Hartung hesitated at the front door. He felt like an ant at a picnic every time he walked into The Hard Time Cafe. Yeah, an ant, he thought, smiling inwardly. Just looking for a few crumbs. Even though trouble was the farthest thing from his mind, his hand automatically went to his right hip, checking for the S&W snub-nose revolver he wore under his jacket. Then, notebook tucked into the crook of his left arm, he put on his official face and went in.

"Oh." Chet Tomzak, the restaurant's business manager, was leaning against the cashier's counter, talking to another parolee who was working the register that day, when he saw Hartung. "Afternoon. You here for lunch or, uh, business?"

"Business, I'm afraid." Hartung didn't recognize the parolee behind the register; he wasn't one of his. But Chet Tomzak was. "Don't worry, Chet, I'm not looking for you."

Tom Hartung was with the state Division of Parole. He was one of thirty-six parole officers assigned to Riverton and the surrounding county. That sounded like a lot to some people until they found out that there were nearly two thousand parolees to keep track of in the county.

Hartung's current case load had him monitoring thirty-four parolees, including about half the men working at The Hard Time. He liked the program and admired the priest who ran it, Father Costello. He just wished they wouldn't all treat him like a leper whenever he visited the place.

"Father Joe around?" he asked. "I checked at the rectory and they thought he might be over here. You seen him?"

"Well, uh, he's around somewhere, I think."

Tomzak and Hartung both looked through the arched doorway and scanned the dining room. Father Joe wasn't among the several dozen men and women who made up the Thursday lunch crowd.

Tomzak shrugged. "I guess he stepped out. Or something."

"Right." Hartung gave him the five-second stare. It was the one he'd perfected after years of standing on stoops all over the city, listening to a parolee's mother or girlfriend try to stonewall him when the parolee wasn't where he was supposed to be. He took out a stick of gum, stripped it, and folded it into his mouth. After chewing for a moment, he said, "How 'bout Sister Matthew, she around?"

"Well, I don't think so. You might check with the church office at the rectory—"

"I did. They sent me here. Next you'll remember they both went on a retreat somewhere in the Poconos, right?"

Tomzak couldn't think of how to respond to that, so he didn't. "Uh, look, why don't I take you back to the office?" he said. "You could wait there, maybe have a bite to eat? On the house, of course. I'm sure Joe'll be along sooner or later."

"Right." Hartung noted that Tomzak didn't ask what this was all about or more specifically who this was all about. Which meant he already knew. But since it was past his lunchtime—"Lead the way, Chet. How are the Big House barbecued babybacks today?"

* * *

"You've got a runner," is all Hartung said when Father Joe finally joined him in the restaurant's cramped office.

"Now, Tom—"

"No, don't jerk me around, Father. It's written all over your face, for Pete's sake. You might as well be wearing a sign. It's Frawlic, right?"

Hartung was leaning back in the swivel chair, a plate bearing the bones of an order of barbecued ribs sitting on the desk in front of him. Father Joe was slumped against the door frame, there being no room for a second chair in the tiny converted storage closet. His bloodshot eyes looked a size too small for their sockets.

He exhaled wearily. "We've been looking for him since last night. He took the church van out for some errands around two yesterday afternoon and never returned."

"And you didn't bother to call me," Hartung said, his mouth a grim line.

A shrug. "I thought if we could locate him—"

"Don't give me that crap. You know I could sink this whole program of yours right now. You've got a legal obligation to report any violations by the men in your charge as soon as you become aware—"

"I know, I know. It was my mistake." Father Joe scratched nervously at his short red beard. "There was a confrontation yesterday between Jeffrey and one of the other men. A personality clash, basically—these things happen. It's just that Frawlic took the worst of it. I expect his pride was hurt and he took off out of anger. Once he's had a chance to cool down, I thought—well, I only wanted to give him every possible chance to come back."

Hartung grunted. "What you've given him is every possible chance to clear the state line before anyone's the wiser." He pulled a palm-size cell phone from his jacket pocket and punched in a series of numbers. After a moment, he said tersely, "This is Hartung with the state P.O. I'm requesting an APB on one of my parolees."

* * *

They were at their favorite table along the left side of the dining room, beside a window that overlooked the alley. Sergeant Hafner sipped his coffee and read the paper while Sergeant Greene worked on a wedge of cheesecake.

"Cheesecake for lunch," Hafner said, not looking up from the paper. "Pretty soon those Italian suits of yours won't fit over the gut you're gonna have."

"Then I guess I'll have to borrow some of your clothes," Greene said.

"Speaking of cheesecake," Hafner said with a smirk. "Your girlfriend certainly got a lot of mileage from recycling those alphabet murders. You see yesterday's paper? Jesus, they gave her half the front page and a whole page on the inside. You'd think it all happened yesterday, not twenty years ago."

"I told you, one dinner doesn't make her my girlfriend. And yes, I did read the article. I thought, all in all, it was a good piece. Very well written."

"Uh-huh. A good piece." Hafner decided against making the obvious comment. "That's why you took a personal day yesterday, right? To get ready for a date that meant nothing to you?" When his partner refused to bite, Hafner asked, "So where'd you take her to dinner anyway?"

"The Rio."

"Whoa. The Rio. *Mucho dinero, amigo.*"

"It's Brazilian, Harold," Greene said around the last forkful of cheesecake. "They speak Portuguese in Brazil, not Spanish."

"Like there's a difference." Hafner had already lost interest in his partner's love life. He pointed his index finger at Greene's chest and made a shooting motion. "I got a bet for you. I'll bet you the check for this lunch that our buddy, Father Costello, has got himself a runner."

Greene frowned and looked around the room. "How d'you figure?"

"We got a bet?"

"No. You're too cheap to bet on anything that isn't a sure thing. What happened, you see something on the warrants list this morning?"

"Uh-uh. I saw something in this restaurant a little while ago. Or some*one*. You know a guy named Tom Hartung? He's a P.O., works out of the division office over on West Main."

"Short, stocky guy? Kinda reddish, curly hair, going bald?"

"That's him. He walked through the dining room with Tomzak about a half hour ago, back toward that office cubbyhole. Tomzak looked like the cat that swallowed the canary. I'll bet you one of Costello's choirboys decided to go solo."

"Now you've got me curious," Greene said, tossing his napkin on the table. "Let's say we go back and find out."

Hartung was just completing his call for an APB when the two detectives crowded into the hall outside the office. Father Joe's reaction at the sight of them, a low groan, could be heard all the way out in the dining room.

From the chair, Tom Hartung looked up and said, "Hey, two of Riverton's finest. And they say there's never a cop around when you need one."

"Who is it?" Hafner asked, not wasting time with chit-chat.

"One of my newbies. A capital offender named Frawlic, Jeffrey John. He missed our appointment this morning. The good Father here tells me he took off in the Corpus Christi van sometime yesterday afternoon. I just phoned it in to Metro."

"I didn't say he 'took off,'" Father Joe protested mildly. "He just hasn't come back yet, is all."

"Uh-huh. Frawlic, Frawlic." Hafner squinted at the priest, then at this partner. "Where do I know that name—?"

"It's the con you thought you recognized when we were in a couple weeks ago," Greene reminded him. "You pulled his sheet, remember? Murder two for cutting his girlfriend's throat. Then he got mixed up in a jailhouse hit, ended up doing almost twenty at Arcadia."

"Yeah, that's right. Frawlic, skinny little bastard with weird eyes." Hafner rubbed at the shadow of beard on his jaw. "Y'know, as I think about it—yeah!" He clapped his hands. "That's where I remembered the guy from, Kel. Your girlfriend's piece on the alphabet murders? I brought Frawlic in for questioning on that case—way back when—me and another uniform named Szminski."

"I didn't think you worked that case."

"I didn't, not really. I was still on patrol in those days, but the task force called in any and all manpower it could for the alphabet murders. Alls we did was go out and pick up a few suspects and leave 'em off for Tony Spola and the other dicks to do the questioning." He looked down at the seated parole officer. "Jesus, and the guy picks yesterday to run? That's interesting, huh?"

But Hartung didn't see it. "What's so interesting about yesterday?"

"It was the twentieth anniversary of the last alphabet killing," Greene said.

"You're not suggesting that Jeffrey Frawlic—" Father Joe began, but Hafner cut him off.

"I'm suggesting it's an interesting coincidence, that's all." With a glance to his partner, he added, "And, like, maybe it'd be interesting to go back to the shop, check to see if any little girls have been reported missing since yesterday. Little girls with double initials."

"Jeez, Hafner, it must be a slow day down at Metro, you're reaching that far for straws," Hartung said. He pushed his fireplug five-foot-six-inch body up from the swivel chair. "What we got here is your basic runner, a dummy who thinks he's a genius. 'Hey! I'll just steal me this nice van and drive down to Florida and live happily ever after.' Like we don't know enough to fax every cop house between here and the sunshine state with a picture and description of this clown." He eased past Father Joe and out into the corridor. "If you guys are really looking for something to keep you busy, c'mon and help me get the word out on Frawlic. Maybe we can get that van back before it ends up in a Miami chop shop."

"Sorry, we don't do lost dogs or straying cons," Hafner said. "Now if the punk assaults or kills somebody, you give us a call."

* * *

As it happened, Greene and Hafner did get the call. It came at ten to five that afternoon, just when they were about to go off duty. Of course, it wasn't until they had driven their unmarked Ford sedan way out to the far end of West Avenue, out near the sprawling warehouse district, that they found out it had anything to do with Jeffrey Frawlic and Corpus Christi's church van. All they knew was that it was a Code 29 call.

Someone had found a dead body under suspicious circumstances.

The crime scene was at the end of Halstead Street, a

dead end flanked by a weedy rail spur on the left and a tall, empty warehouse building on the right. An ugly street leading nowhere, making it a perfect spot to ditch a hot car or a dead body. Or in this case, one of each. Two blue-and-whites and the green hearse from the Medical Examiner's Office were already there. They were parked in a loose semicircle around a white Ford Econoline van, the stretch version with tinted window glass on all sides.

Neither detective recognized the van right away. Other than a small cross on the special-issue license plate, there were no markings to identify it as the Corpus Christi van.

Greene found a spot for their car and parked at an angle to the curb. As the two men got out, a blue-and-white mobile unit from the department's forensics lab pulled onto the street. It was followed closely by a local TV news team in a loud red Chevy Lumina.

Greene looked back over his shoulder at the TV crew and glanced at his watch. "Great. Forty-six minutes till airtime, which means they'll be bugging us for details we don't have and ambushing us with a live remote."

"Ain't technology grand?" Hafner said. He led the way under the yellow crime-scene tape and located the uniformed officer who had called in the Code 29. He was a young one, maybe twenty-six or -seven. He looked a little nervous but under control. This wasn't his first stiff, Hafner judged.

"What's the story, uh, Clymer?"

"Well, I was on routine patrol and saw the van parked down here all on its own, so I decided to check it out. You know, run the plate, see if it was hot. And it was—a church van reported stolen this afternoon. So then I pulled up and looked in and saw the body—"

"Whoa! This is the Corpus Christi van?" Hafner gave it another look.

Greene had already figured that out, having noticed

the cross on the plate. While his partner was talking to the young patrolman, he had walked around to the other side of the van, where the M.E. was checking over the body. Now he came back around to join Hafner.

"I'll bet you a lunch Father Costello doesn't have a runner anymore," he said.

Hafner blinked. "You mean—?"

"Somebody put an extra hole in Jeffrey Frawlic's head."

Chapter 9

It appeared to be a .38-caliber hole. Possibly a nine millimeter, the medical examiner's assistant said. Also the body's temperature and condition suggested the victim had been dead for at least sixteen hours.

"Maybe more."

"How much more?"

"Like twenty-four, maybe even longer. These cool October nights screw up the science a little. We'll know a lot more after the autopsy, naturally."

"And when will that be?" Sergeant Hafner wanted to know.

The M.E.'s assistant scratched a dry patch of skin at his receding hairline. "*That* I wouldn't wanna even guess at. There's also some facial bruising, but that looks like it occurred earlier. A few hours, anyway."

"You mean somebody beat him up, then came back later and shot him in the head?"

"He was punched around and he was shot, detective. But not at the same time. More than that I can't tell you until after the M.E.'s report."

They let him get back to the gruesome work of tagging and bagging the late Jeffrey Frawlic. Sergeant Greene looked to his partner expectantly. They both knew what came next—canvassing the neighborhood. "We'll wanna grab a few more uniforms to help out," he said.

"Yeah." Hafner looked over his shoulder at the huge empty warehouse. "I guess I'll take a guy with me and check out that building. Maybe a derelict saw something. You wanna do the houses down at the other end of the street?"

Greene nodded. "We'll have to do the side streets later too."

"Yeah." Hafner shook his head wearily. "Guess I better call the wife, tell her not to wait supper. Again."

* * *

It took more than two hours to do a preliminary canvas of the neighborhood, and all they came up with was a shortlist of long shots.

Somebody saw a tall black male in shabby clothes come down the street the previous afternoon carrying a garbage bag over his shoulder. Probably a guy collecting returnables, but Greene made note of it anyway. Somebody else remembered an old white man shuffling along sometime in the late afternoon or early evening on Wednesday. Two elderly women reported seeing a "suspicious" car on the street around five o'clock.

"It looked like a pimp-mobile, long, shiny, and champagne colored," one of the old ladies whose hair was an impossible shade of red had told Greene in a stage whisper.

He had written that down too, but now, comparing notes with Hafner, he said, "I got a feeling our perp didn't come back into the 'hood driving a pimp-mobile. Especially not a couple hours after the victim probably died."

"I don't know. Say he wanted to check on his handiwork, like an arsonist coming back to watch the fire."

"You're not serious. Sticking out like a sore thumb in a flashy car?"

"Prob'ly not." Hafner shrugged. "Anyway, if there *was* somebody in a car, it probably means we've got a pair of killers working together. One to ride over here in the van with Frawlic and the other to drive the car. But somehow that don't sit right with me."

"That there was a second vehicle or a second killer?"

"Neither one, really. This just feels like a personal revenge thing to me." He shrugged again. "It's just a feeling, but I mean—one in the side of the head? It's almost like it's a mob hit."

"Actually, the personal revenge approach makes sense," Greene said, glancing back over his shoulder at the van. "It wasn't car theft. And Frawlic wasn't robbed—his wallet and about fifteen bucks were still on him. And the guy *was* an ex-con, which means he probably pissed off more than his share of people in his day."

The candidates, they both knew, would include anyone from a relative of that girlfriend he killed way back when to some other con with a grudge against Frawlic.

"Yeah, and there's the bruises. Say Frawlic has a beef with somebody, maybe one of the other cons, in the morning. They fight. The other con gets in a few licks, but he wants more. So a few hours later he takes a ride with Frawlic and finishes him off."

"Okay. But if there was only one killer," Greene went on, "how *did* he get away from the scene? You think he's living in this area? Drove the van over here because it was convenient for him?"

"Maybe. On the other hand, we're only three long blocks west of Dewey Avenue. That's a trunk line for the

RTS. If he grabs a bus and a transfer, he could've gone from here to anyplace in the county and then some."

The two detectives looked at each other for a moment, each reluctant to state the obvious. It was already seven o'clock. Beyond the arcs of the streetlamps and the yellow glows from nearby houses, the neighborhood was dark and quiet. The October air was chilly and damp. Little would be gained knocking on any more doors that night in that neighborhood; they could re-canvass in the morning, if necessary.

But there was one door, across town, that they could knock on that night.

* * *

Hafner said to Father Costello, "You ever consider changing the name of this church to Corpus Delecti?"

Father Joe didn't even try to humor him. "You think this is funny, Sergeant? A man's been murdered and you're making jokes?"

Hafner ducked his head sheepishly. "Sorry, Father. Occupational hazard. When you investigate murder for a living, it gets to be routine, like anything else."

They were in the rectory in the front parlor. Father Joe had taken a seat in a wing chair next to the massive fireplace. Greene sat on the edge of the worn leather sofa while Hafner paced the hardwood floor. On a butler's table between the chair and sofa were coffee and cookies provided by Mrs. Clooney. They were untouched.

Greene filled the silence that had overtaken the other two men with a simple declarative sentence. "We need to know which of your parolees had it in for Frawlic, Father."

A protest was halfway out of the priest's mouth, but he bit it back. "All right. I think I already mentioned that there'd been some bad blood between Jeffrey and one of the men."

"This bad blood—it was a fistfight, right?"

"Some punches were thrown in the heat of the moment. One of the men has some history with Frawlic, and I'm afraid it boiled over yesterday morning. But I'm sure he had nothing to do with this murder—he's not a killer, gentlemen, not even in his old life was he into violence. I can understand why you need to—"

"The name, Father." Hafner had quickly overcome his embarrassment and was back to his usual self. "You can be a character witness at the trial if it comes to that. Right now, we're already twenty-four hours behind the killer and we're just beginning our investigation. Time is of the essence as they say, okay?"

Father Joe leaned back in his chair and exhaled. He had arguments to make, defenses to raise, but he knew the sergeant was right. This wasn't the time or the place.

"The man you want to talk to, gentlemen," he said, keeping his voice casual, "is Reuben Macky."

* * *

"I'll cut right to the chase, Macky," said Sergeant Greene. "Where were you yesterday afternoon between two and four o'clock?"

The three men were crowded into Macky's room like the proverbial bulls in a china shop. It was a small space to begin with, perhaps twelve by fifteen feet. A door led to a tiny bathroom. There was a kitchenette along one wall and an unmade double bed along another. In between was a battered oak pedestal table where Greene and Reuben Macky sat.

Hafner remained standing, leaning against the door leading to the hallway, hands in the pockets of his raincoat. He was absently whistling a Sinatra standard, "The Best Is Yet to Come."

Father Joe had given up Macky's name at around eight. It was now nearly ten. Hafner and Greene had spent more than an hour chasing down and interviewing

Sister Matthew. Then they had grabbed coffees and danish at the shop down the block from The Hard Time Cafe, waiting. When Reuben Macky and Chet Tomzak came out of the cafe around nine-thirty into a cold drizzle, the two detectives met them on the sidewalk.

"What's it about?" were the first words out of Tomzak. And the last.

"Just a few questions for your buddy here," Hafner had told him. "It's no big deal, so don't try to turn it into one." To Macky he added, "You got someplace dry we can chat, Reuben? Like maybe you'd like to invite us up to your place?"

Macky thought about it a couple of pregnant seconds, looking for options that weren't there. Then he said, "Sure. Why not?"

In the harsh light from the room's only lamp, Macky's dark face looked as gray and weathered as old barn wood. His cafe uniform of blue jeans and blue cotton workshirt smelled of cigarette smoke and french fries. It had been a long day at the restaurant and he'd been looking forward to a hot shower and a cold bottle of beer. Now all he wanted was to get the two cops out of his room and out of his life.

"I was working at the restaurant most of the day, but I took a break around two-fifteen," he said, drawing on a Kool. "Look, you guys wanna tell me what's—"

"Your pal Jeffrey Frawlic turned up dead," Hafner said.

Macky took a moment to digest the news. He shook his head slowly. "Imagine that. And they say only the good die young."

"We knew you'd be busted up about it."

"You want me to pretend I liked the little bastard?"

"We don't want you to pretend about anything, Reuben," Greene said. "How long was your break?"

"About an hour."

"An hour?" Hafner snorted. "Jesus, you guys think you work for the feds?"

"Must be contagious. You don't look like you've missed many lunch hours, Hafner."

"Oh, it was your lunch hour. So where'd you go for lunch?"

"I didn't." He pulled on the cigarette. "You work in a restaurant, you nibble all day. Last thing you wanna do on your break is eat. I went for a walk mostly. And I sat on a bench over near the fountain in Lafayette Square."

"You sat around in the rain?"

"It wasn't rainin' at the time, man."

Greene said, "You know anybody who can vouch for you for the time you were out of the restaurant? You see anyone you know in the park, maybe?"

"Couple of pigeons I feed regular, is all."

"He thinks it's funny, Kel. He thinks we're here to entertain him." Hafner crossed the room and kicked a spare chair away from the table and sat down on it. Macky was bigger and wider than he was but not by much. And Hafner had the extra weight of his badge going for him. He leaned in close.

"Let me tell you what I think went down, Reuben, baby. Just so you'll know I'm deadly goddamned serious here, okay? I think you hated Jeffrey Frawlic's guts on account of he was a slimy little ratbag who set up a buddy of yours in the joint. You couldn't stand the sight of him working around the cafe, driving the church van around like some hot shit, like he *belonged*. Even gave you some lip, didn't he? Pissed you off so bad you knocked the little squirt around a bit."

Macky blinked slowly and crushed out his cigarette, keeping silent.

"The way I see it going down," Hafner went on, "you'd had enough of Frawlic after your run-in yesterday. So right around the time he was supposed to leave, you decide to take your lunch break. You get out to the van a few minutes before he does and you hunker down in the back, in the cargo area behind the last seat."

Macky smiled. "You see me hunkerin' down in that little space, do you?"

"Oh, you'd fit. All you'd need was motivation, and you had that. The punk gave you lip, and then Sister Matty put you down for beatin' on him, didn't she? And in front of all your homies at the restaurant. Oh, yeah, I think you were plenty motivated."

Macky shook his head but didn't say anything. It had been years since he'd been questioned by cops, but he hadn't forgotten how it worked. If they had solid evidence, they came in guns high and ordered you face down on the floor and cuffed you. If all they had was a theory, they came at you with questions, hoping to goad you into making their case for them.

Greene, talking like he was just making conversation, like this was just between a couple of brothers, said, "So what'd you cap him with, Reuben, a .38? Maybe a nine? You got yourself an auto tucked away in here someplace, man?"

"I don't have no guns, here or anywhere else."

"You mind if we take a look for ourselves?"

"Don't you need a search warrant for that?"

"Not if you give us permission, Macky," Hafner said. "You invited us up here, right? So why don't we keep the whole thing on a friendly basis?" After a beat, he added, "You got nothin' to hide, do you?"

Macky waved his hand. "Go right ahead, gents."

The two detectives looked at each other. They both knew this was too easy. If there ever was a gun, Macky hadn't been stupid enough to bring it back to his room. But they went ahead and tossed the place anyway.

Chapter 10

"Look, I didn't kill him. God knows I hated him, but I didn't have anything to do with his death. I swear it, Joe."

"I know that, Reuben. We all know that." He looked to the others for support.

"We're on your side, man," Billboard said, and Chet Tomzak nodded in agreement.

"I appreciate that, I really do. But it's those two homicide cops I need to convince, and they ain't buying."

"Come now," Sister Matty chirped. "Enough with the doom and gloom. You have to look on the bright side. After all, they didn't arrest you, did they?"

"Not yet they haven't. But they will."

"But you're innocent."

That got a snicker from all the parolees seated around the table.

"Like that makes a difference to a couple of cops," Macky said.

"Of course it makes a difference, " Father Joe protested. "Sorting out the guilty from the innocent is what they do."

"Oh, man." Billboard rolled his eyes. "The only two innocents I know are you and the Sister here. Look, lemme explain somethin' for the both of you. A cop's job ain't to arrest the guilty, it's to arrest *somebody. Anybody* who fits the bill. And then leave it to the lawyers to make a case out of it."

"I think you're being cynical, William," Sister Matty said. She turned to Chet Tomzak. "Chester, what do you have to say?"

"Well—" He hesitated. He knew what she expected him to say. After all, he was the college guy, the only ex-con in the room who hadn't been a career criminal before going to prison. His crime had been vehicular homicide, resulting from a single night of too much booze and far too little judgment. In theory, he hadn't been in the system long enough to become jaded. But she was forgetting the experience he'd had with Hafner and Greene only six months earlier.

He decided to remind her. "What did they have on me, Matty, when they pulled me in after Father Joe was assaulted? No proof at all, except that I was in the right place at the right time. And I was an ex-con."

"But you were never charged—"

"No. But I probably would've been if you and I hadn't gone out ourselves and proved my innocence."

"There's that word again," Macky said, reaching for his pack of cigarettes. "The fact is when the cops make up their minds about a suspect, that's it. They don't go lookin' for any other possibilities. They just put all their time and manpower into building a case on that one poor slob."

It was Friday morning, some two hours before the restaurant was due to open for the lunch trade. They were seated around the large table in the center of the dining room. Macky lit up and blew a smoke ring toward the ceiling, trying not to let his nerves show through. All around the room, the framed movie posters from popular prison movies seemed to mock him.

"Well," Sister Matty said, thinking it out, "we simply need to do it again."

"Do what?"

"Become proactive. Find a reason for the sergeants to look for other suspects, is what I mean. Provide them with some good leads."

Billboard grunted. "What the hell? I guess somebody's got to do their jobs for 'em."

* * *

Meanwhile, back at their desks at Metro HQ, the sergeants in question were reevaluating.

"What we've got is entirely circumstantial, Harold. The DA's office wouldn't give us the time of day— which, coincidentally, is all we've got on Macky. He was away from work and unaccounted for when the shooting went down."

"*And* he had motive, don't forget. He hated Frawlic; he beat him up. Even threatened to kill him." Hafner swiped a hand across his face. He'd had six hours of sleep, which wasn't bad, but he still felt as if sand fleas had dug in at the corners of his eyes. Middle age sucked.

"But I know what you mean, Kel," he conceded.

"On paper Macky looks like our man, only we got no physical evidence."

Greene adjusted the knot of his paisley silk tie. "I suppose there's always the chance we're taking the wrong angle here. Maybe it really was just a simple carjacking, only something went wrong, Frawlic got himself shot, and the hijacker got spooked and took off. I mean, if I was trying to boost a car and ended up killing the driver, I'd walk away. Forget the car and the guy's wallet—I wouldn't want anything to do with it."

Hafner chewed on that a few seconds, nodding slowly. Then, "Nah. It still smells like a revenge killing to me. Of course, that don't mean it has to be another ex-con who did Frawlic. Like you said, Kel, the guy most likely pissed off lots of people in his time."

"Yeah, like the family of that girlfriend he killed. What was her name?"

Hafner pulled a piece of paper out of the litter on his desk and squinted at it. "Natalie Abramowitz, age 19 at the time. A cleaning woman."

"So you're ahead of me already."

"Just standard ops, partner. We always check out the relatives of the victim when a perp gets popped."

"You come up with anything on Abramowitz's family yet?"

"Some names and addresses we'll need to check out. But first I wanna go over this Tech Unit's report, see if there's something in here." He slapped at the copy of the report that had just been dropped onto his desk. "Maybe the techs got lucky going over the van."

"Yeah, right." Greene began leafing through his own copy. "Like maybe Macky left behind a couple of big thumbprints and some saliva on a stick of ABC gum in the ashtray? The problem with that is it wouldn't matter if he did. No doubt Macky's ridden in that van lots of times. Doesn't mean he was in it on Wednesday afternoon, as any defense attorney worth his salt would quickly point out."

Hafner muttered a profanity and shoved the report aside, reaching for a paper cup of lukewarm coffee to console himself with. His partner, however, continued to browse through the pink pages of the Technical Unit's report.

"Y'know, there was something bothered me about that Frawlic creep from the beginning, Kel. Remember? How I zeroed in on the little ratbag that day at the restaurant? I knew I'd seen him before."

"Mmm." Greene nodded, but kept reading.

"And then remembering how I knew the guy, from that old alphabet murder case? And on top of that, the ratbag gets himself offed on the twentieth anniversary of the last murder. I mean, don't you find that a little too goddamn coincidental for comfort, Kel? Kel?"

"Hmm?"

"The alphabet murders. I was half blowing smoke yesterday when I played up the possibility to Frawlic's parole officer, but now—I don't know. Maybe it's an angle we oughta look at. Kel? What, I'm talking to myself today?"

"I heard every word. What's more, I agree with you." He looked up. "You and that old cop mentor of yours—"

"Tony Spola."

"Yeah, Spola. You guys said a piece of evidence that turned up at each of the crime scenes was withheld from the press, to help weed out the sickos who kept calling in to confess. You recall what it was?"

"Sure. The cat hairs. They found cat hairs on each of the victims, and only one of the little girls kept a cat in the house. They figured it was how the killer lured his victims, showing them a kitty. Nice world, huh?"

Greene held up the report and tapped a finger against an item listed on the second page. "We got cat hairs, Harold. In the van and on Frawlic's clothing."

* * *

"Okay, so we need to come up with some leads to force-feed the cops," Macky said. "But how do we do that? Like, where do we even start?"

Sister Matty's thinking process hadn't gotten that far yet. Luckily, Father Joe's had. He raked the fingertips of his right hand through his beard. "You know, when they were here yesterday talking with Tom Hartung, Sergeant Hafner made some interesting comments. He suggested the possibility that Jeffrey Frawlic may've been connected with that old murder case, the alphabet murders."

"Oh, dear." Sister Matty made a hurried sign of the cross. "Those poor, poor children. I read the article in the paper the other day—as much of it as I could take."

"Yeah, it's enough to make you sick," Macky said. "Wouldn't surprise me in the least if that little weasel Frawlic was involved."

"But so what if he was?" Tomzak wanted to know. "I mean, what help is that to us?"

"It means, Chester, that perhaps someone connected with that old case went after Jeffrey. Someone who believed he was the killer and has been waiting all these years for revenge." Matty nibbled nervously at her lower lip. "Of course, without access to the police files on the case, it won't be easy to track people down after all this time."

"Yeah, and how happy do you figure those two cops will be to share those files with us?"

Father Joe cleared his throat. "There *is* an alternative source of information, people. Someone who's had recent access to all the old police files. The reporter, the one who wrote the anniversary piece—what was the name?"

* * *

"L. J. Trudeau could be a problem."

"Lena?" Greene's left eyebrow shot up. "How'd you figure she's a problem?"

"Not just her, but the media in general," Hafner said.

"Mm. You're right. If the newshounds hear we're looking into the alphabet murders, it'll be like the second coming of O.J. and the white Ford Bronco."

"So we gotta proceed with the utmost caution. Keep our mouths shut."

"Right."

"Especially you."

"Me?"

"Well, I sure as hell ain't the one sleeping with a reporter."

"And neither am I!"

"Yeah, well, one more dinner at the Rio and you will be."

"Hey, screw you, Harold."

"That'd cost you at least three dinners."

"Which in your case amounts to a Big Mac, a Whopper, and a pizza from Barbones." Greene scooped up an empty paper coffee cup and flipped it at the trash basket, rimming out.

Hafner considered making an observation about racial stereotyping, but decided to restrain himself. Instead, he stayed on topic. "I'm just saying, if your Miss Trudeau hears about—"

"Don't, Harold. You've made your point, okay? Now just leave it alone."

"Fine." Hafner shuffled a few papers, then glanced up. "One last question?"

Greene stared for a full three seconds before saying, "What is it?"

"I was just wondering, you don't talk in your sleep, do you?"

Chapter 11

The newsroom at the *Riverton Times-Democrat* was roughly the size of a football field. Down the center, tan desks with fake wood tops were butted together in twos and fours. Along the sides were cubicles of varying sizes. They were for the assistant metro editors, the wire room, business and sports, and so on.

The middle of the room was for the metro reporters. Most of the desks were crowded with piles of paper surrounding well-used video display terminals. Lena Trudeau's was no exception. She was pounding away on her VDT's keyboard when Sister Matty and Reuben Macky found her.

"Goodness," Matty said, after the introductions went around. "It's so quiet in here. I expected, I don't know, lots of bustle and chaos."

Lena surveyed the half-empty newsroom. "We're a morning paper, which means we work late into the night.

You want to see frenzy, Sister, come back in about twelve hours when the first deadline hits."

"The first deadline?"

"There're three in all: ten-thirty for the regional edition, midnight for the metro, and one A.M. for the sunrise edition."

"And each edition is different?"

"Usually. The front pages, anyway, depending on late-breaking national and local stories. We try to be as timely as we can be, but it's tough when you've got to compete against twenty-four hour cable news stations. Of course, everything's computerized these days and that's a big help."

Macky hadn't followed a word. He was still taking in the young woman's casual smile and deep hazel eyes. She was wearing a long skirt and a cable-knit sweater that was too bulky to give away much of her figure. She caught him appraising her and called him on it.

"Do I pass muster, Mr. Macky?"

"Call me Macky. Or Reuben. Just so's you call me." He grinned at her. "And yes, ma'am, you pass just fine."

After grabbing a chair from another desk, Sister Matty brought the talk back around to Jeffrey Frawlic. She had explained briefly about his murder over the phone earlier that morning. Now she filled in the rest, including Macky's unfortunate tie-in. She ended with their suspicion that Frawlic may have been connected with the alphabet murders.

"Wow," the reporter said. "And the cops on the case make the same connection?"

"That's how Father Joe first heard of it. Sergeant Hafner mentioned that Jeffrey had been questioned in the alphabet murders twenty years ago and—"

"Wait a sec, did you say Hafner? Are Hafner and

Kelvin Greene working this case?"

"Yes. Is that important?"

Lena smiled. "Good sources are always important, Sister." She snatched the phone set and punched in a number from memory.

* * *

Hafner was down in records, looking for some missing pieces of information. Greene was still at his desk, compiling a list of names and addresses from the old files. When the phone bleated, he grabbed it and cradled it under his chin like a violin.

"Greene speaking."

"Good morning, Kelvin." Her voice was a purr soaked in cream.

"Hel-lo there." Greene sank back into his chair, his voice dropping into his Barry White mode. "You beat me to the punch. I was gonna call you later, see if you could make dinner tomorrow night. Assuming I can get away from work long enough for a night out."

"Oh, things are busy down there? Did you catch an important case?"

"Uh, well, I wouldn't say important. Necessarily. A homicide."

"Yeah? Tell me more. Is this something I might be interested in writing up?"

"You? I doubt it. I mean, you might wanna give it a few paragraphs at some point, but we're just getting going on it."

"Uh-huh. Would this be that ex-convict who was found murdered in the church van last night?" Lena asked, innocent as a newborn, adding, "Our night cops reporter filed something on it."

Greene's delivery stiffened a touch. "Yes. Yes, that's the case. An ex-con named Frawlic, one of Father Costello's guys over at Corpus Christi. We're thinking it may've been another con that did it, a grudge that carried over from Frawlic's prison days. But don't quote me on that, Lena, okay? It's too early yet—"

It's later than you think, she thought. Time to get down to business. She cleared her throat and lowered her voice an octave. "Listen, Kelvin, I have a source who says Frawlic is connected to the alphabet murders. That you guys are looking into the possibility that he *was* the alphabet killer—"

"Jesus Christ, where'd that come from?" Greene sat up straight. "I told you, we're just getting rolling here, but we're looking at this as a simple revenge deal—"

"Right. Revenge by one of the family members of one of the little girls who were murdered by him twenty years ago—"

"No! No, I said we're looking at another ex-con because of something that went down at Arcadia back about seven, eight years ago." Greene attempted a chuckle, while at the same time wiping away a bead of sweat. "You know what I bet happened, Lena? Your source got mixed up. See, Harold's got a secondary theory, that maybe a relative of the *girlfriend* Frawlic murdered back twenty years ago has been waiting for him to get out. I think your source heard that twenty years part and remembered your story on the alphabet murders. He put two and two together and got five."

"That's what you think happened, huh?"

"Absolutely."

"So you're not looking into any alphabet murders angle? Scouts' honor?"

"Scouts' honor, I swear. At the moment, all we're checking out is those two angles I mentioned, a revenge killing by another ex-con or possibly a family member of Natalie Abramowitz. That's the girlfriend Frawlic murdered."

"Uh-huh." Lena decided not to pursue the qualifier—"at the moment"—but she had heard it. "By the way, Kelvin, were you ever a scout?"

* * *

She recradled the phone and said, "You'd think a cop would be a better liar, wouldn't you?"

"What'd he say?"

"A lot of lawyerly denial, basically. What it boils down to is they're probably looking into the alphabet murders angle, but they don't want the media getting in the way. So he's stonewalling."

Matty said, "You're not angry? I mean, you have a friendship with this man, and yet he lies to you—"

"This is business, Sister. Sometimes it's his job to, let's say, avoid the truth. Reporters do the same thing sometimes, although for different reasons." She winked. "Now if he lied to me about a personal matter, that would be different."

Macky fidgeted on his perch on the corner of her desk. "Not that this isn't interesting, ladies, but can we move on to the reason we came by? We figured if we clued you in to this alphabet murders connection, you'd be grateful enough to give us some information. Like the names and how to reach folks you interviewed for your anniversary story."

"I'd be glad to, but—" She thought about it for a moment. "The problem is there are so few people with any direct knowledge of the case. I know it's only been twenty years, but I was amazed to find how many key people had died."

"For instance?"

"Well, almost all of the detectives who led the special task force. Really, only Tony Spola is alive and well.

There's another retired cop, Lou Carragio, who's in a nursing home suffering from Alzheimer's. Just about all the other important police sources are dead."

"What about the relatives of the victims?"

"Mm, that's even worse. It's downright spooky how many of the victims' family members have either died or gone nuts or simply moved away."

Matty said, "I remember in your piece you quoted from the father of one of the dead girls—"

"Stanislaus Cazminski. His daughter Catherine was the third victim." Lena's shoulders shivered beneath the sweater. "There's an interview I wouldn't want to do over. It was like when I was back writing obits—obituaries—on the night rewrite desk. Only ten times worse."

"The man is still in mourning for his child?"

"Yes, if anger and guilt can be considered mourning."

"They can," Sister Matty said. "Tell us about Mr. Cazminski. The quote you ran seemed mild enough. Something about how he thought of his daughter often."

"'When she was alive I didn't pay enough attention to her,' he said. 'But since she died I've thought of almost nothing and no one else.' I had to reconstruct that quote after the interview. The truth is Mr. Cazminski went ballistic and ordered me off his property. He's a haunted man, filled with rage."

Macky made eye contact with Sister Matty, who was thinking the same thing. Anger that could burn that hot for twenty years could easily lead a man to murder.

Macky said to Lena, "You got an address for this Stanislaus Cazminski?"

Chapter 12

"Explain to me again why we're schlepping out to Greenwood instead of working the alphabet killer angle."

Greene steered the unmarked Ford to the off-ramp of the 390 expressway. "Because we're establishing a logic table. First we looked at Reuben Macky, who's still a possible. Then we checked out Frawlic's immediate kin, of which there's only his mother. She's too old, too frail, and too sick to have killed anyone even if she wanted to. So scratch her. Now we need to look at relatives of the girlfriend Frawlic murdered, see if we turn up anything there. And this brother, Neil Abramowitz, is our best bet, so—"

"Yeah, yeah, Neil Abramowitz made threats against Frawlic at the trial, how he was gonna get him for killing his sister. But that was twenty years ago. He was a seventeen-year-old punk with a juvie record. And I still don't see why we have to work this angle over the alphabet killer angle, logic table or no logic table."

"It's just a way of rank ordering the investigation, Harold. If we rank each suspect group according to likelihood, I just think the family of the girl we know Frawlic murdered ranks higher than relatives of girls he may *possibly* have murdered."

Greene snuck a peek to see if his partner was still buying it. In truth, he'd talked Hafner into following up the Abramowitz angle first so that he could later tell Lena Trudeau he hadn't lied to her. Not technically, anyway. So far, they weren't investigating any connection between Jeffrey Frawlic and the infamous alphabet murders. With any luck, maybe they wouldn't have to.

But he couldn't tell Hafner his real reason, not without letting him know that Lena had heard about a possible connection to the alphabet murders. And he wasn't about to do that since Hafner would accuse him of being Lena's source. So he had used some buzzwords from his college criminology courses to explain himself. He knew Hafner hated it when he did that.

"Well, I know one thing," Hafner said as he merged with the crawl of traffic on Jefferson Boulevard. "No matter which end of this investigation we start at, my weekend out at Hamlin Beach is shot to hell. Unless we get super lucky and close this thing out today, which ain't even on the radar screen."

Hafner was a camping enthusiast if living out of a twenty-two-foot RV with microwave oven and color TV can be called camping. Hamlin Beach State Park, up along the lake, was one of his favorite spots, Greene knew. Still, he asked, "A little late in the season for camping, isn't it, Harold?"

"Nah, October's one of the best times. You got your leaves changing colors, good crisp weather for hiking or fishing, crackling bonfires at night. And no crowds. Just you and the family." His standard frown deepened. "Not that Marie or the kids are that big on it. Marie'd just as soon stay home and doodle around the yard, I think. And Rob—" His oldest son. "—we couldn't even get him to come along on the summer trip down to Gettysburg. Girls and hot rods, that's all he ever thinks about anymore."

"What sixteen-year-old boy doesn't?"

"Yeah, I guess. Thank God Petey's only eleven. He still likes getting out into the woods with the old man."

Greenwood was a close-in suburb on Riverton's west side. The parts of town that weren't four-lane highways lined with shopping strips were cookie-cutter housing developments. The one Neil Abramowitz lived in was called Westway Estates. It was a collection of small post-war Cape Cod and ranch houses built on a grid of narrow streets with cute names. Abramowitz's "estate" was at 19 Sunnyside Lane.

"Jesus," Hafner muttered, pulling up in front of the place. "Looks like the yard sale from hell."

It was a Cape Cod-style house with green asphalt roofing and white vinyl siding that needed a good powerwash. The attached garage, two and a half cars wide, was almost as big as the house itself. Parked in the crumbling driveway was an old spotty GMC pickup truck. The yard was littered with for-sale items including a motorcycle missing a wheel, a flatbed trailer, and a wooden box crammed with hubcaps.

The entire mess was surrounded by a rusting chain-link fence that sported Beware of the Dog and No Soliciting signs.

"I don't see a dog," Greene said, looking the yard over carefully as they climbed from the Ford. He had a thing about dogs, especially the kind people buy to guard crapholes like this. "Place like this always has at least one, though."

"Tell you what, Kel," Hafner said as he opened the gate and headed up the walkway, "if one of these piles of junk moves, shoot it."

They made it to the front stoop without any problems. Greene was on the alert for a growl or a large water bowl, even a pile of dog crap someplace, but there was nothing of a canine nature anyplace. "Maybe they figure the sign was enough, huh?"

Hafner pressed the doorbell, surprised to hear that it actually worked. He lay on it for a few seconds until he could hear a deadbolt being slid back on the other side of the door. It swung inward, revealing a man in his mid- to late thirties. He had brown hair and dull brown eyes, half closed. His moon face sported a two-day growth of whiskers. He was wearing a frown along with drooping jeans and an oversized Dallas Cowboys jersey that failed to conceal a large beer gut.

"Yeah? What the hell—?"

"Metro PD," Hafner said, holding up his shield. That got the man's attention; his eyes shot wide open. "Are you Neil Abramowitz?"

Before Hafner could get the last syllable out, the door slammed shut in his face. Both cops reflexively moved to either side of the door and put their hands on their weapons. From inside came the sound of pounding footsteps and overturned furniture.

Greene said, "I'll take the back—you go call for backup."

"Right."

By the time Hafner reached the Ford and Greene made it into the overgrown backyard, Abramowitz—if that's who he was—was leaping the side fence. Greene sprinted after him, taking the fence in one bound like the hurdler he'd been in school. Abramowitz had already moved on to the next yard and was moving across it like a halfback through a crowded backfield. Greene was faster and fitter, but his quarry knew the terrain.

Barking.

Greene had been gaining on Abramowitz, but now he stopped suddenly at the next fence. He could hear a large dog barking, but he couldn't see it. Couldn't see his man, either, but then Abramowitz ran out from behind an aboveground swimming pool. He shot through a stand of yews, disappearing into the next yard. Greene hesitated a moment longer, still hearing the dog closeby but not seeing it. Then, with a gulp, he leaped the fence and ran a zigzag across the yard. The dog, a big rottweiler, came at him from behind the pool.

"Christ!" Greene felt the blood drain from his face as the dog leaped at him. But it abruptly stopped in midair and yelped as it crashed to the ground. It was chained.

"Thank you, Lord," Greene muttered as he charged through the stand of yews.

Hafner, meanwhile, was driving down Sunnyside Lane with one hand while calling in for backup with the other. He hung a right at Hillendale Circle, scanning the yards until he spotted Abramowitz crossing between two houses. Hafner slammed on the brakes and skidded to a stop. Hopping out, he drew his 9 mm pistol and lined it up across the hood of the Ford. Just then, Abramowitz stumbled through a boxwood hedge and out onto the street.

"Gotcha, shitbag."

Abramowitz, panting, half raised his arms in surrender. Then he leaned over and threw up all over his shoes.

* * *

While Hafner and Greene were busy in the suburbs, Sister Matty and Reuben Macky were in Dutchtown, tracking down Stanislaus Cazminski. Father Joe was driving them, using his own car, a Honda Civic. The church van was still impounded down at the Metro garage.

"Are you sure she said 43 Forest Avenue?" Father Joe asked.

"Yes, positive. This must be it."

"Guy lives in a meat market?" Macky said.

"A former meat market." The building was shuttered with a sun-faded real estate company sign in the dusty window. "Maybe there's an apartment unit in back, off the alley there. There often is with places like this."

It was an old-fashioned brick and glass storefront, a boxy rectangle. It obviously had been added on many years before to the front of a Victorian-era house. What had once been the small front yard was now taken up by the store and half a dozen parking spaces.

Father Joe decided to stay in the car while Sister Matty and Macky checked around back for an apartment. They walked up a service sidewalk along the side of the building. In the back were a porch and an entry door and, beside the door, two door buzzers. Sure enough, the lower one had a yellowed name tag taped over it: Cazminski.

"Well," Matty said hesitantly. "I guess this is the place."

"Yeah." Macky reached past her and pressed the buzzer. "Lemme ask you something. Now that we're here, what're we supposed to do? Ask the guy if he blew away Frawlic?"

The little nun had been silently asking herself the same question. It had seemed like the natural thing to do back at the newspaper: track down relatives of the alphabet killer's victims and question them. And then—?

"In the movies, a few hard questions and some deductive reasoning is all it takes," she said.

"Right. Except this ain't the movies, Sister, and I'm not even sure what *deductive* means."

"Leave the questioning to me," Matty said, sounding much more confident than she felt. "You just stand there and look, uh, supportive."

"I can do that."

They heard footsteps and the metallic sounds of chains being unhooked and deadbolts unlocking. Then the chipped door opened, revealing a tall, very thin man who looked as yellowed as the name tag on the door. Long, oily, gray-streaked blond hair; faded blue eyes deepset in a lined, sallow, stubbled face; an odor of cigarettes confirmed by the yellow teeth and nicotine-stained fingers. His age could've been anywhere from fifty to seventy.

"Hell you want?" His voice was a rasp, his breath eighty-proof.

"Mr. Cazminski? My name is Sister Matthew—"

"Yah? And who's this, Brother Remus?"

Macky began to surge forward, but Matty blocked him off without ever losing eye contact with Cazminski.

"I'm with Corpus Christi Church, Mr. Cazminski. My associate here, Mr. Macky, manages our restaurant operation—"

"The Pope know you're out dressed like that, huh?" He looked disdainfully at her khaki pants and hooded

Fordham sweatshirt. "They ruint the church with that Vatican II is what they did. Not even a Polish pope could fix what they done." A trace of an accent came through the slurred words. "Now, I think you and your blackie better go away—"

This time Macky reached past Matty, catching the edge of the door as Cazminski attempted to slam it shut. A hard shove sent both the door and the man back in the other direction. Cazminski fell backward onto the floor of the grimy foyer, stunning himself when his head banged against a cast-iron radiator.

Sister Matty went to one knee and looked him over as he lay there moaning. "He'll be all right. It's the alcohol that's got him befuddled as much as the fall." She rose. "We should take him into his apartment. Why don't you go and get Father Joe—"

"I can carry this guy myself."

"I don't doubt it, but we need Father Joe to question him. Maybe the sight of his clerical collar will succeed where my trousers and sneakers haven't."

* * *

She was right; one look at Father Joe's priestly garb and Cazminski calmed down. Thank goodness Father Joe hadn't opted for jeans that day, as he often did.

They had carried the groggy man into the apartment and deposited him on a beatup sofa. *Beatup* was the key word for the whole place. Overstuffed furniture that hadn't been replaced since the Sixties; a faded Oriental carpet on the floor; an odor of stale smoke everywhere from the heavy drapes to the discolored wallpaper. An empty whiskey bottle lay on its side on a coffee table strewn with newspapers.

While Matty was in the kitchen boiling water for instant coffee, Father Joe took a chair opposite Cazminski. Macky stayed in the background, leaning against the apartment door, his huge arms crossed. A few reassuring words from Father Joe had gotten Cazminski talking.

"It wasn't always like this. Back in the Sixties, before the neighborhood went—" He stole a glance at Macky. "—downhill, it was a decent enough place to live. Me and my wife, Sylvie, ran the meat market up front there. It's true, we had some hard times. I—I left the family for a time, Father. I was young then and I drank too much. Sylvie threw me out, and she and Cathy had to go on welfare for a little while. I'm so ashamed—"

"It's okay, Stanislaus."

"But I came back, and it was going to be all right again. Sylvie forgave me. I stopped drinking and running around. But then, that's when . . . when . . ."

Father Joe said gently, "When your daughter was taken from you?"

"Yah, when our little Cathy was m-murdered. I thought I was being punished by God, Father. For a long time, I was so angry at Him—"

"He understands, Stanislaus."

"Sylvie and me, we were empty people after that. The business got worse and worse, until we had to close it down and I went to work for Wagers." A large supermarket chain. "Then Sylvie died two years—no, three years ago." He looked up with those runny, faded eyes of his just as Matty slipped into the room with the coffees.

"I been drinkin' extra heavy the last couple of days.

Don't ask me why," he said, matter-of-factly. "I always thought I'd be happy, everything would be okay, once that son of a bitch was dead."

Father Joe's jaw dropped. Matty almost dropped the tray. Reuben Macky dropped the cool pose and arched his eyebrows. All three followed Cazminski's shaking finger as it pointed to a section of the newspaper that lay atop the mess on the coffee table.

Circled in blue ink was a headline that read: Ex-con Found Murdered in Execution-style Slaying.

Macky caught the eye first of the priest, then of the nun, and said, "Bingo."

CHAPTER 13

"I told you, the dog slowed me down."

"Uh-huh."

"You should've seen it."

"I've heard so much about it in the last hour, I feel like I have."

They were back at Metro HQ, sipping coffees in Styrofoam cups outside Interview Room 3. Inside I-Room 3 waited Neil Abramowitz in a clean pair of tennis shoes, looking not so much scared now as simply bored. And defeated.

"You believe this nitwit?" Hafner said, watching him through the one-way mirror. "Taking off like that because of a garage full of hot auto parts? Christ, if he keeps his cool and answers a few questions, we're outa there without suspecting a thing."

"Well," Greene said, "the house was full of stuff too. I don't know about you, Harold, but I think a living room coffee table stacked with used carburetors would've got me thinking."

"Yeah, I guess there's no way he could let us in the house without blowing it."

As soon as he found out the two cops suspected him of murder, Abramowitz had confessed to the auto parts theft. "I didn't kill nobody, man," he said repeatedly on the ride in. "But I'd put a medal on whoever did. Frawlic killed my big sister, man. He should've fried."

They didn't just take his word for it, naturally. But it turned out he had an alibi for the afternoon of the murder. While Jeffrey Frawlic was taking a bullet to the brain, Neil Abramowitz was being ticketed for speeding on the state turnpike, some two hundred miles from Riverton. He still had the ticket in the glove compartment of his car, and a call to the state troopers had verified the citation. Now they were waiting to turn Abramowitz over to a couple of detectives from the Property Crimes Unit.

Hafner took another sip of coffee. "I guess, according to the old logic table, it's time we moved on to the alphabet murders angle, huh?"

Greene couldn't disagree, much as he might've wanted to. "Problem is, the files are full of holes. I mean, half the stuff seems to be lost or misfiled. And what's left you either can't read or it doesn't add up to much anyway."

"That's the basic flaw in your department-wide task forces, particularly under the old, pre-computers filing system. Cops ain't that great at filling out all those reports. Especially when they know the investigation's dead-ending," Haefner said.

"That's why I was thinking maybe we should go to the horse's mouth, so to speak. I mean go talk to your buddy, Tony Spola. Maybe he can point us in the right direction."

"Yeah. At the very least he should know what they had on Frawlic that made him a suspect in the first place." Hafner drained the coffee and tossed the cup. "Tell you what, Kel. I'll go look up his address, you go down to Supply and get yourself a can of pepper spray."

Greene frowned. "What for?"

"Just in case Tony's got a dog."

* * *

Stanislaus Cazminski held up his trembling hands. "If I could hold a gun with these, I still wouldn't have shot the bastard. No, if I had the chance—the courage—I would've chop, chop, chopped him up like a side of beef." He banged the edge of his right hand on the coffee table to demonstrate. "Cut him into pieces like the animal he was and feed him to the dogs. That's what I wished I could do to Jeffrey Frawlic."

"So—you're saying you didn't kill him?"

"You wanna give me the credit, I'll be proud to claim it. I'm sorry, Father, but that's how deep my hatred goes." He shook his head. "But I didn't kill him. I wish I did, but I didn't."

Sister Matty urged him to drink his coffee, but he waved her away. He was still groggy or half drunk, or perhaps this was a permanent condition. Perhaps too many years of drink and anger and pain had made him punch-drunk. His attention seemed to wax and wane like the tides.

"Mr. Cazminski," she said, touching his arm. His head came up. "How do you know about Jeffrey

Frawlic? I mean, after so many years, what makes you suspect that he was your daughter's killer?"

He stared at her, some of the anger boiling to the surface again. "How'd I know? Twenty years ago, they arrested him for killing my little Cathy and those other poor girls, did you know that?"

Father Joe said, "We understood that he was *questioned* about the case, Stanislaus, but never charged—"

"Charged? Ahh, so he wasn't charged, but he was the one. I *saw* him parked out on the street, right out here on Forest Avenue, the day before our Cathy was taken. He was in a hippie van, orange with a big yellow sun on the side. I saw him from inside the shop, out there watching the little kids walking home from school at St. Kazimir. This is how the police found out about him in the first place, because I *saw* him. But—they let him go." He threw himself back against the sofa and closed his eyes.

The others were silent for a few moments. Macky was the first to speak.

"Like the man says, I doubt he could even hold a gun straight. I'm sorry to say it, because I thought for a minute there I was off the hook with the cops. But this ain't no killer. What we got here is a bitter old man, been chewing on a piece of hate for twenty years with no place to spit."

"I think you're probably right, Reuben," Joe said quietly. "We can give his name to the police, let them look into it a little deeper. But I can't see this man stalking Jeffrey—"

"Wait a minute," Matty cut in, her brow furrowed. "We're missing something. Something he said before about—'I've been drinking extra heavy the last couple of days.' Something like that. You remember?"

"Yeah, so? He was talking about yesterday and today. Frawlic was killed on Wednesday. This guy hears about it the next day on the news and goes on a binge."

"Jeffrey Frawlic went *missing* on Wednesday, but no one knew about it except those of us at Corpus Christi. His body wasn't found in the van until last night. And this newspaper item—" She snatched up the paper and held it up for all to see. "—didn't appear until this morning. So how did Mr. Cazminski *know* about the murder yesterday?"

"Because, little Sister," came a rasping voice from the depths of the sofa, "he called me and told me."

Father Joe and Matty rushed over and nudged and pulled Cazminski into a sitting position. His head lolled sideways like a rag doll's.

"Who told you about the killing, Stanislaus?"

"I want a drink. Gimme another—"

"No, you don't need a drink. You need to tell us who called you about Jeffrey Frawlic."

"*He* called. My guardian angel. Been calling for years and years, keeping me informed." He belched, and his eyes popped open. Suddenly he seemed lucid again. He shook his shoulders, blinked a couple of times, and said, "What're you people doing in my house? I don't want you here. Get out!"

"Mr. Cazminski, you were telling us about your guardian angel. Someone who called to let you know about Jeffrey Frawlic's death?"

"Ah, ah, ah." He wagged a finger, then stumbled to his feet. "Forgive me, Father, for I have sinned, and I'm about to sin some more. I got another bottle in the back, see?

So you take your coffees and you get the hell out, okay? That's all I got to say to you."

* * *

Tony Spola had retired to the small town of Derry, about a twenty-minute expressway ride from downtown Riverton. Greene and Hafner made it down there in the middle of the afternoon. It was a beautiful, crisp October day, and the gentle hills surrounding the village were brilliant with fall color.

"Nice day for it," Greene said.

"Yeah. Would've been a great weekend for camping," Hafner said. "Listen, when I called Tony? He sounded really tired, probably that heart condition of his. If I start to get long-winded with stories about the old days, you get me back on track, okay? I don't wanna take up too much of his time."

When Spola greeted them at the front door of his neat colonial house, he indeed looked gray and tired. It had been little more than a week since they'd seen him at lunch at The Hard Time Cafe, but he seemed to have aged several years. He could read the concern in their eyes.

"My Lord, I don't know if I should even let you in. You boys are looking at me like a couple of pallbearers."

"I'm really sorry to be taking up your time, Tone. I only—"

"Get in here, Haffy, and quit worrying about it, for pity's sake. I'm an old man with a bum ticker, and one of these days I'm gonna keel over and die. Okay? Now that we've got that out of the way, let's move on."

They did, as far as a pair of matching club chairs in the cheery living room. It smelled of lilacs with an undercurrent of cigarette smoke. The retired cop eased himself onto a corner of the couch and picked up a pack of Camels from the end table. He caught the look on Hafner's face as he lit up.

"The wife gives me a hard enough time," he growled. "Gotten so I can't hardly enjoy a smoke unless she's gone shopping, which is where she is now. So don't you go and try to spoil my fun."

"It's your funeral."

"Exactly." He took in a lungful and sighed. "All right, boys. What'd you wanna see me about?"

"About a creep named Jeffrey Frawlic. Ring any bells?"

"Sure, distant bells. He was one of the suspects we hauled in on the alphabet murders. I think a witness spotted him hanging around the Cazminski girl's neighborhood the day before she was taken. In a stand-out vehicle, a custom van or something. Anyway, we ran him down, did a background check as usual, and had a couple uniforms bring him in for questioning."

"I was one of the uniforms," Hafner said.

"That I didn't remember."

"I'm surprised you remember Frawlic so well after all this time. You must've questioned, what? Fifty suspects in all?"

"At least, although some were better possibilities than others." He took another puff, then rested the butt in an ashtray. "Wait here, boys. I'll just be a sec."

Slowly he got up from the couch and crossed the living room. A short hallway led past the kitchen to a small den at the back of the house. A old oak desk and chair, a pair of file cabinets, and a beatup upholstered chair were the only furnishings. Spola was flipping through one of the file folders on the desk when Hafner appeared in the doorway.

"You need a hand, Tone?"

"You mean an arm?" he grumbled. "The old bastard can't even walk thirty feet without falling down, is that what you mean?"

"Sorry, Tony. I just—"

"Forget it. I've got file copies on most of the key stuff from the alphabet murders in here some place. Biggest case me and Ben Garfield ever had. If I can just find that damn report—"

He went back to rummaging through the desk. Hafner, meanwhile, couldn't help but notice the heavy smoke odor that coated the room. The nicotine staining was so bad on the walls, he could see the ghost outlines where pictures or other items had once hung. This den had to have been the old cop's hideaway for many years, Hafner thought. The place where his wife would leave him be to smoke his Camels and relive his old cases.

"Ah, got it." He held up a thin set of papers. "Let's go get comfortable again, huh?"

Back in the living room, Spola put on a pair of reading glasses and slowly scanned the pages he held in his lap. "Mm, uh-huh. Here it is. Day and time of the Jeffrey Frawlic interview nearly twenty years ago to the day. Yeah, here's your name, Haffy, as one of the escort officers."

He looked up. "Truth is, I was going through the old files this morning, trying to find out what I could about that interview way back when."

"Oh, yeah? What got you interested all of a sudden?"

Spola smiled slyly. "Article I saw in the paper. I see an item about an ex-con who was found dead and right away the name jumps out at me. It's always like that for me. Give me a name that goes back twenty, thirty, even forty years, and if the guy was dirty, I remember him."

"Yeah, I'm like that too, only with faces."

"Anyway, boys, as I remember, Frawlic was a decent suspect at the time, and believe me, we were hot for decent suspects. Only he didn't pan out for some reason—" He seemed to drift off for a moment, then his head came back up and he snapped his fingers. "Right. This is the guy whose girlfriend alibied him for the time span on the third murder. So we had to spring him. The crazy part is, he later got into a fight with the girlfriend and killed her, so he ended up in Arcadia anyway."

"Didn't you have anything else on him, Mr. Spola?" Greene asked. "I mean, besides his vehicle being seen in the vicinity of the third victim's house?"

"Call me Tony. Well, really all we had besides proximity to one of the victims was that he basically fit the FBI profile. He was the right age, the right race, the right what they call socio-economic background. He had the right sort of low-level, low-esteem job, clerking at a convenience store. He was a loner, and people who knew him said he was antisocial. It all fit the profile, for whatever that's worth. But at the time, it's about all we had to work with, so we used it."

"So that's really all there was? The vehicle ID and the FBI profile?"

"Well, there was the numbers and letters deal. Frawlic had some strange fascination with letter and number combinations, according to some folks who knew him. We thought that fit pretty well with the killer's apparent fascination with victims who had double initials."

"I'd say so," Hafner nodded. "But you couldn't put together a case—?"

"There's dozens of people in this area who're into numerology and such. And we had absolutely no physical evidence connecting Jeffrey Frawlic—or anyone else—to any of the murders." He put down the file and picked up the cigarettes. "Listen, are you guys gonna let me in on what's going on here?"

Hafner started to speak, but before he could say anything, the phone rang. Spola picked it up, said hello, and listened intently for a minute.

"Yes, I see," he said. "Well, that's possible, I suppose. You could come out for a few minutes this afternoon. All right then. Good-bye."

"Well, well, well," he said, hanging up the phone. "Isn't that interesting. Miss L. J. Trudeau wants to interview me again. She seems to think you boys suspect this Jeffrey Frawlic may be our long-lost alphabet killer. How about that?"

Greene looked sheepishly at Hafner, who looked back at him and muttered, "Shit."

CHAPTER 14

From the backseat of the Civic, Sister Matty leaned forward and said, "What could he have meant, that someone's been keeping him informed 'for years and years'?"

Father Joe, making eye contact in the rearview mirror, said, "Obviously it means someone who's followed the case has kept in touch over the years. Apparently someone who finally decided to take action against Jeffrey once he got out of prison."

"But what I don't understand is, what's there to keep track of? As you say, Jeffrey was in prison all those years. He couldn't be a worry or a threat to anyone until—"

"Until he got out," Macky said, half-turning in the Honda's cramped front passenger seat. "Parole hearings, that's gotta be it. Frawlic must've had at least six or eight parole board reviews while he was inside. This 'guardian angel' of Cazminski's must've been keeping him informed of the outcomes. Maybe he was even appearing at the hearings, giving statements against Frawlic's release."

"Yes, yes," Father Joe nodded. "And they keep records of these hearings. You've seen the stenographers, Sister, remember? Goodness knows, you and I've attended enough parole reviews together over the years."

"Okay, great. Now, what do they do with these records?"

"I don't know, but I'll bet a copy of each parolee's file goes to the local office of the state Division of Parole," Macky said.

And they all three said as one, "Tom Hartung!"

* * *

The Division of Parole shared a midtown office building with half a dozen other state agencies. Hartung's office was part of a fifth-floor complex that housed thirty-six parole officers. As a senior man, he qualified for a window overlooking West Main and enough floor space for two guest chairs fronting his desk. That left Reuben Macky standing, at his own insistence.

"So. To what do I owe this surprise visit? Don't tell me—you've come to apologize again for giving me the runaround on Jeffrey Frawlic. Well, don't sweat it, Father. I've decided not to report that little oversight."

Father Costello leaned forward in his chair, genuinely grateful. "I can't tell you how much I appreciate that, Tom, truly."

"But that's not why we're here," Macky said bluntly.

Hartung didn't like sitting while others stood. It accentuated his shortness, for one thing. It also gave the other person a bird's-eye look at the thinning hair atop Hartung's head. And he didn't like parolees with attitudes. He gave Macky his best cold stare, but it didn't faze him. Macky knew Hartung couldn't touch him; his parole period had officially ended a few months earlier.

Hartung sighed. "Okay, then. What's up?"

Father Joe took the lead. "You know about Jeffrey Frawlic's murder."

He was well informed, naturally, on the Frawlic matter. It had been a bit of a shock at first, yes. But truth be told, he'd been relieved when the liaison officer over at Metro had called to give him the news. Frawlic's death swept under the rug any blame that might have come Hartung's way for letting him run in the first place. It also reduced his caseload by one, which was always a welcome development. Of course, it wouldn't do to let them know that.

"Yes, I was sorry to hear about it. I didn't know Frawlic all that well yet, still I was surprised. He was so quiet." A little candy ass, is what Hartung was thinking. "I thought he was one of those one-timers who'd stay out of trouble when he got out of prison. Although, in this case, I guess it's more like trouble found him. A carjacking gone bad would be my guess."

"Yes," Father Joe said. "Well, it's starting to look a little more complicated than that."

He spent the next few minutes explaining everything they knew or suspected about the case. When he told about Macky's history with Frawlic, Hartung's furry eyebrows rose. When he got to the part about Stanislaus Cazminski and his "guardian angel," they collapsed into a V. When Father Joe finished his recital, Hartung was wearing his bulldog frown.

"The alphabet murders—who'd a thunk it." He looked up at Macky. "Of course, the ramblings of an old drunk don't mean much. Unless you've got more than you told me, you're still the prime suspect."

"We're working on it."

"And I suppose that's where I come in?"

Sister Matthew couldn't hold back any longer. "Yes, Mr. Hartung, that indeed is where you come in. You see, we think this guardian angel of Mr. Cazminski's must be someone who has followed Jeffrey's parole hearings over the years. Quite possibly it's someone who has attended and perhaps even spoken out at the hearings. Someone who strongly opposed parole."

Hartung shrugged. "It could be somebody who just wrote letters. Usually in capital cases or sex crimes they get lots of letters. You know, from relatives of the victims and victims' rights groups."

"In any case, wouldn't there be a record of all that? Letters, testimony?"

"Sure. You know how government works. We've got records of everything in triplicate. The originals would be filed in the state capital at the department's Board of Review for Pardons and Parole."

"The originals," the nun said, cocking her head. "Which implies there's another set of records somewhere—maybe locally?"

"Of course. The parole officer assigned always gets a complete packet on a new parolee. I got Frawlic's about two weeks before he was released. I reviewed it—" Skimmed it anyway. "—then sent it down to Records for filing."

Sister Matty exhaled. "Can we see it?"

"Sure," Hartung said, his face impassive. "It's a public document."

"Great."

"First you'll have to file a formal request with the Board of Review for Pardons and Paroles. That'll take a few weeks to work its way through the state bureaucracy. And there's an administrative fee of sixty dollars. If you want a tip, pay with a money order instead of a personal check, to speed up—"

"Wait a damn minute," Macky said. "A few weeks? All we wanna do is take a look at some public records, man."

"Right, and I'm telling you what you need to do." *Man.* Hartung hated when they called him that. It showed no goddamned respect whatsoever. He aimed a finger at Macky. "A society has rules and we have to follow those rules. That's a lesson I thought you would've learned by now."

"There's no need to get testy, gentlemen," Matty said.

"Look, Tom." Father Joe casually rested an elbow on the edge of Hartung's desk. "I know all about procedures and paperwork, believe me. The church has no end of hoops for me to jump through with all the programs we run at Corpus Christi. But you know what I've learned over the years?"

"What's that, Father?"

"I've learned to tell the difference between a necessity and a formality." A smile parted the neat red beard. "I'm sure you've done the same."

"There are times—" Hartung allowed. Then, with a steely glance at Macky, he added, "But I'm basically a by-the-book man, Father. I keep my nose clean and I expect others to."

"Uh-huh." Father Joe sat back. A slight change of tack was in order. "This book of yours, Tom. Does it say anything about accepting gifts, say free meals, in the performance of your duties? Because I'm guessing that sort of thing would be frowned upon, officially speaking."

"Well, uh, that's sort of a gray area—"

"I'm glad to hear that, Tom, because we enjoy your visits to the restaurant. And we know how much you enjoy a plate of ribs or a club sandwich. On the house. I'd hate to see a friendly tradition like that stopped on account of an overly strict enforcement of the rules."

Hartung's mouth began to water at the mere mention of The Hard Time Cafe's Big House barbecued babyback ribs. "Nobody's trying to be a hard-ass here, Father."

"Naturally not." Joe put his elbow back on the desk. "You had a good Catholic-school education as I recall, Tom. You must've had some Latin training?"

"Yeah, two years. I was an altar boy, y'know."

"Excellent. Then I'm sure you understand the meaning of a *quid pro quo*."

Hartung looked from the priest to the nun, who was grinning, to the ex-con, who wasn't. Then he went back to the priest. "You're slicker than frozen spit on a sidewalk, Father Costello, y'know that?"

"Can we see the Frawlic file?"

Hartung picked up the telephone and punched in three numbers. After giving instructions to the person on the other end, he hung up and said, "There's a small conference room one floor down, room number 412. They'll bring you the files there. You can't take them out of the building, okay? If you need copies of something, call my extension, 336."

After they left, he sat back for a moment and stewed. Then he picked up the phone again and got an outside line. There was one other thing the book required of him in a case like this, and he intended to see it got done.

After several rings, a heavy voice on the other end said, "Metro PD, Hafner speaking. How can I do you?"

Chapter 15

"My God!"

Sergeant Kelvin Greene skimmed the last page of the last notebook. Then he flipped it shut and shoved it across the desk with the others. It was one thing to suspect Jeffrey Frawlic was the notorious alphabet killer. It was quite another thing to come face to face with proof of his guilt.

On the way back from Derry, the detectives had finally gotten around to visiting Frawlic's residence. It was deemed a low priority since the crime had been committed elsewhere. Therefore the room had been locked up the night before by police order, but no search had been made.

It was a single room with a shared bath over off Carson Avenue. The minute the landlord let them in, Greene knew they had walked into something unusual, something evil. The stillness of the room. The bareness. The yellow light that edged in through the drawn blinds.

The shivering chill of the place, like an empty meat locker.

He told himself he was being foolish, letting his imagination rule.

Then Hafner had found the box of notebooks under the bed.

There were an even dozen of them. Common spiral notebooks, each containing perhaps one hundred sheets of white, lined three-hole paper. The kind of notebooks carried by millions of little kids all over the country, which only made these even more obscene. At first glance the pages seemed filled with gibberish. Line upon line of numbers and letters, letters and numbers. No rhyme or reason that they could see. They repacked the box and took the whole works back down to Metro HQ.

It was there, at their desks, that the detectives began finding the bits of information that condemned Frawlic.

Greene was the first to notice that not everything in the notebooks was nonsense. There were chapter numbers, and at the beginning of each chapter was a recognizable name or phrase. "Corpus Christi Catholic Church," for example. The words were spelled out in large block letters at the top of the page. Immediately below, also in block letters, were the initials C-C-C-C. Below that were 3-3-3-3, followed by the notation, "Four 3s, a quad set, means luck in all four seasons!" After that came three full pages of letter and number combinations that meant nothing, as far as Greene could tell.

Some of the chapters began with dates: Frawlic's birth date, the date of his release from prison, some dates that had no clear meaning. Others began with names, including Reuben Macky and some other names Hafner and Greene recognized from The Hard Time Cafe. Under Macky's name, Frawlic had printed out "Big Bad Black Bastard" and "Nothing to fear, his hate does not influence our fate.

Mission okay." Two pages of letters and numbers followed.

But it was the last of the notebooks, the one that was less than half filled, that proved the clincher. One of the chapter headings read "Kitten," and was followed by a series of scratched-out names and numbers and letters. It ended with the name "FLUFFY" written out in bold block print. Another chapter began with the date of the twentieth anniversary of the last alphabet murder, "October 10"—the day Frawlic would die. Below it was what looked like a license plate number: "4D7 J3F." On a hunch, Hafner checked it out and wasn't surprised to find it was the plate for the church van. The only other notation that made any sense to the two detectives was the line, "Perfect symmetry for mission."

Finally, there was the chapter headed by a name. "Dinah DiMaria." The double initials leaped off the page at Hafner, and he felt the acids churning in his stomach. Below the name, and preceding page after page of nonsense letters and numbers, was this: "At last, Sacrifice Four is close enough to taste."

After showing the last notebook to Greene, Hafner said, "Whoever killed this bastard did the world a favor."

"Yeah. I guess there's not much doubt now. Jeffrey Frawlic was the alphabet killer."

"And he was about to do it again. How much you wanna bet if we check the city grammar schools, we come up with a ten-to-twelve-year-old girl named Dinah DiMaria?"

That's when Hafner's phone rang. While he took the call, Greene went back to checking the notebooks, until he'd had enough of Frawlic's mad doodling.

Hafner recradled the phone. "I'll tell you who that was if you promise not to alert the media."

Greene simply stared across the desk. He wasn't in a

guessing mood, and he'd already taken enough crap about Lena Trudeau.

"Hartung," Hafner said. "Frawlic's parole officer? Seems he's got a crew of amateur sleuths over there. Our friends from Corpus Christi, Father Brown, Miss Marple, and—what's a good name for a black private eye?"

Greene said, "How 'bout Sam Spade?"

Hafner laughed. "I'm glad you said that and not me."

* * *

The amateurs were just then examining an inch-thick file folder. The tab on the folder read "Jeffrey Frawlic," followed by a date of birth and a prison ID number. Inside were pink and yellow and white sheets of paper. These were copies from review board reports, photocopies of letters, copies of prison fitness reports, and so on.

"We'd better divvy these up," Father Joe suggested, handing a stack each to Sister Matty and Reuben Macky.

Fifteen minutes went by with only the occasional grunt, usually followed by "What?" and the reply, "Nothing." There were a few letters from family and friends of the woman Frawlic had been convicted of killing, Natalie Abramowitz. The earliest letters, sent at the time of Frawlic's first parole hearing, were angry and emotional. They were also the most numerous. In the years after that first hearing, letters became fewer and began to sound like form letters. Like people going through the motions.

The victim's brother Neil Abramowitz had written once, early on, but that was it.

It was in the pink sheets that Sister Matty found the clue they were looking for. These were copies of the official review board reports. There were seven such reports in all, reflecting the seven times Frawlic had been up for a parole hearing.

"Anybody know what AO stands for?"

Macky moved his chair closer and read over her shoulder. "Hmm. Arresting officer?"

"That makes sense, given the stuff written in under 'Comments.'" She did some more reading. "I suppose it's no surprise that the policemen and prosecutors who put a man away wouldn't want to see him get out any too soon."

Macky grunted. "Or at all."

"Mm. It seems odd, though—how many arresting officers would there be normally?"

"One or two, I guess. How many you got?"

"Looks like four different names. And this last one, he reminds me of something, but I can't—" Then she got it. "Father Joe!" She grabbed the priest's arm. "At Jeffrey's final parole review, that man who was seated behind us. The one who spoke against his release! Remember?"

Father Joe's mouth fell open. "Of course! He was the same man who—" He jumped up and clapped Matty on the shoulder. "I think you've just uncovered our 'guardian angel.'"

* * *

"You ask me," Tom Hartung said, elbows resting on his desk, "it sounds like a case of good riddance to bad rubbish. Maybe you guys should take a holiday on this one, huh?"

Hafner and Greene ignored the comment.

Knowing that Jeffrey Frawlic had been a sadistic serial killer was beside the point. The two very different policemen would continue to pursue the case, although for two very different reasons. For Greene it was the law; a society must live by the rules it makes for itself. For

Hafner, it was the job; somebody was trying to get away with murder. That's what it came down to. Everything else was for DAs and judges and juries to decide.

"Where've you got the meddlers?" Hafner asked him.

"I don't. You guys took your sweet time getting over here—"

"Wait a minute, what d'ya mean you don't?"

"That's what I'm telling you, Hafner. When I called you, they were downstairs in a conference room going over Frawlic's parole file. But they found something they liked and had me make some copies. Then they took off."

"Took off where?"

"I got no idea." Hartung shrugged. "Look, I did the courtesy of calling you guys to let you know a suspect in a homicide was over here checking out a file. But don't expect me to sit on 'em for you. We got enough of our own to babysit."

Hafner looked angry enough to swat the smug look off the parole officer's face, but Greene stepped in.

"Show us the Frawlic file," he said to Hartung. Looking to his partner, he added, "If those three could find anything significant in that stuff, we can too."

"Yeah," Hafner said. "You'd think so, anyway."

CHAPTER 16

The woman who came to the door was old, but still pretty in a weary way. She greeted each of them with a puzzled smile, but it was the priest who held her attention.

"Well, I suppose it's your husband we came to see, ma'am," Father Costello said after the introductions.

"I'm afraid he isn't here just now, Father, although he should be home soon. It's just about suppertime." Worry lines creased her forehead. "We aren't parishioners at Corpus Christi. Could you tell me—what's this visit about?"

"We have a prison outreach program at the church," he said. "There's a restaurant operated by the men—"

"Yes, I read an article about it." She smiled. "The Hard Time Cafe."

"Yes. At any rate, ma'am, one of our men, a parolee named Jeffrey Frawlic—"

At the mention of his name, she breathed in sharply. Her eyes pinched shut for a moment, then she stepped back. "Please. Come in."

She led them into the living room. Matty and Father Joe settled on the couch while Macky took one of the upholstered chairs. She took the other. On the wall behind her chair was a hand-carved teak crucifix with two dry palm fronds slipped in behind it. It was the only embellishment on any of the light green walls. The smell of roasting chicken seeped in from the kitchen.

"Mrs. Spola," Father Joe began, "you were startled when you heard the name Jeffrey Frawlic. Can you tell us why?"

She exhaled. "Oh, where do I begin? I should tell you I don't follow the so-called hard news. It just doesn't interest me, so much sadness in the world. I didn't even know that man had been killed until the reporter came by here an hour ago. Truth is I didn't even know he was out of jail yet—"

"Excuse me, ma'am, did you say a reporter came by? Would that be Miss Trudeau from the *Times-Democrat*?"

"Yes, she came by to talk to Tony about Frawlic. He didn't want me listening, so he had her take him down to the coffee shop in the village. That's where he is now. No doubt smoking away and drinking too much coffee." She stared down at the lap of her housedress, smoothed some imaginary wrinkles. "He thinks I don't know anything about Jeffrey Frawlic. As if he could be obsessed with someone all these years and his own wife wouldn't figure it out."

"What is it exactly that you figured out, Mrs. Spola?"

She hesitated for the briefest moment. She shouldn't be telling tales to strangers, she knew. But it was a burden she'd lived with for so long. And this was a priest, after all. She'd spent her entire life confiding in priests.

She said, "That Jeffrey Frawlic was the man Tony

believed was the alphabet killer. An unsolved case he worked on twenty years ago—and that's been working on him ever since."

Sister Matty said, "That's why he appeared at several of Jeffrey's parole hearings over the years, wasn't it? To encourage the review board to keep him in prison."

"Yes, that had to be it. He never explained any of it to me, of course. He always felt he had to separate his home life from his work, since way back when he was just a patrolman. So as I say, I didn't know this Frawlic had been released, let alone that he'd been—" Her brown eyes suddenly widened. "My Lord, you suspect Tony had something to do with this man's death?"

"We don't know, ma'am. We're simply looking for answers, and they've led us here."

"How? Why?"

Father Joe, with an assist from Sister Matty, explained the series of events that had brought them to the Spolas' living room. At the mention of Stanislaus Cazminski and his "guardian angel," Mrs. Spola closed her eyes and began to cry softly. Father Joe moved over beside her chair to comfort her. Just then, the doorbell rang and Macky answered it.

Hafner and Greene. They joined the others in the crowded living room, Hafner in his old, tan trenchcoat, Greene wearing a dark olive Burberry raincoat. Hafner looked as grim as the slate-gray skies outside.

"Mary, I'm sorry about all this," he said. "To have all these people traipsing into your home like this—"

"It's all right, Harold. At least it's good to see you again. It's been too long."

"Yeah. Somebody's funeral, I think, was the last time."

"Sergeant," Father Joe said. "The reason we drove out to see Mr. Spola—"

Hafner glared at him. "We know why you're here. We saw the names on the parole board records."

A tired voice came from the back hallway. "I knew those records would trip me up sooner or later."

All eyes turned to Tony Spola. He looked about to collapse, and he knew it, offering no protest when Macky took his arm and helped him to a chair. He had walked back from the village coffee shop, he explained, hoping to keep Lena Trudeau and her questions away from Mary.

"Little did I know there'd be such a reception committee waiting for me."

"Tony," Mary Spola said, looking at him with red-rimmed eyes. "They've been to see Stan Cazminski."

"He told us about his guardian angel," Father Joe explained, as much for the two detectives as for Spola. "Someone who had kept him informed about Jeffrey Frawlic's parole status. And who called to let him know Jeffrey was dead, hours before the police found the body in the van."

"Poor Stan. We were parishioners together at St. Kazimir's for years before moving out here. I can still see his daughter Cathy's little blond head sticking up from a pew. I always felt guilty when I'd see him in church after she was killed. That I'd had to let Frawlic go in the alphabet murders case. I figured the least I owed him was to—"

Hafner said woodenly, "Tony, before you say another word, I think I'd better advise you of your rights."

The wizened old cop barked out a laugh. "My rights, Haffy, that's rich. I've got a diseased heart. I'm too far gone even for any kind of bypass surgery—wouldn't survive an operation, the doctors tell me. If you think you can find a judge who'll put me on trial—in six months or a year from now—go ahead."

"It's true," Mary Spola sniffed. "He still smokes and drinks coffee and eats the wrong foods, like he's hurrying himself to the grave."

"I'm a realist is all. And I'm not gonna give up life's last few pleasures just so I can wheeze my way around the house for an extra year or two." Defiantly, he reached into his shirt pocket for his Camels. But seeing his wife's anguished look, he put the pack back.

"Well, Haffy, do you wanna hear my story or don't you?"

Hafner didn't; at least, part of him didn't. That part wanted to go away and leave his old mentor alone for what was left of his life. But the other part of him, the cop part, had to stay. So he Mirandized the old man anyway, and he took out his notepad, and he listened along with all the others.

"Me and my partner, Ben Garfield, weren't many years away from retirement when the alphabet murders went down. We were senior investigators, and this was the biggest case we ever had. It always upset us that we couldn't close it out. So after we hung up our shields, we kept our hands in, ya know?"

"You investigated on your own?"

"Not so much investigated." He held his hand up, palm down, and waggled it. "More like we kept tabs on suspects. Guys we liked for the murders, but we couldn't prove anything. Basically we had two good possibilities in mind from the hundreds who got looked at when the investigation was active. One was a guidance counselor at the school two of the girls went to, a fella named Trisp. Mainly we liked him because he had opportunity, he was a loner, and he was into mathematics. Also he wasn't very cooperative in our interviews. Anyway, him I've kept one eye on for twenty years, just in case. But he's stayed clean as far as I could ever tell. But this other momzer . . ."

"Jeffrey Frawlic."

"Right. When we first picked him up for questioning back on the Cazminski case, he looked good for it," Spola said. "He fit the personality profile, he was seen hanging around, he had this weird thing about letters and numbers. He even kept a cat."

"But his girlfriend, Natalie Abramowitz, sprung him, right?"

"Yeah. Provided him an alibi for the hours the Cazminski girl went missing." He shook his head. "Of course, she was lying for him. And it eventually cost her her life. I figure she knew what Frawlic was up to by then, maybe threatened him with it. Anyway, a couple months go by and he kills her to shut her up."

"But you still suspected him, even after she alibied him?"

"Yes and no. We were looking at so many suspects, Frawlic got forgotten for awhile. But then he came up for killing Natalie Abramowitz. In preparing for the trial, the prosecutor found out that Natalie's cleaning job placed her at the Department of Social Services once a week. We missed that connection when we had Frawlic in for questioning. But now we knew he had a way to get the girls' names—from the AFDC files.

"That made Jeffrey Frawlic a prime suspect again in the alphabet murders. But there still was no real evidence linking him to the case. In the end, the prosecutor and the cops leading the task force decided to take what they could get. Send Frawlic up for the murder of Natalie Abramowitz and keep him in prison for as long as possible."

Hafner nodded. "Initially, the two arresting officers in the Abramowitz case would appear at Frawlic's parole hearings to speak against him. That was Lou Carragio and Sam Jeffries. Then Jeffries died and Carragio got too old and sick to go, so—"

"So Ben went up to one of the reviews, but then he died and I took over. I'd go up and take the board members aside. Do anything I could to spike Frawlic's parole," Spola said.

"He helped me out by gettin' involved in that gambling-debt hit with the Aryan Brotherhood. That earned him another five years. They could've held him for at least two more, but—" He shrugged. "—I lost some of our allies on the review board to retirements. The new ones decided it was more important to free up crowded prison space than to listen to an old man's murder theories."

Green had been letting his partner run with it, but now he picked up the ball. "Once Frawlic made parole, you began keeping tabs on him on the outside?"

"As best I could. It was when he got ahold of that church van that I knew something was gonna happen. He needed wheels, y'see, to abduct little girls."

"That's why you were having lunch at The Hard Time Cafe the day we spoke with you," Greene said. "You were keeping an eye on Frawlic."

"Sending a message. He knew me from all those parole hearings. I wanted him to know I was still watching him." His wrinkled face fell. "It didn't do much good, though. He went right out and found himself another little girl to defile."

Hafner said, "This would be Dinah DiMaria?"

"I didn't know her name myself or how he got it," Spola said. "I just started following that van around every afternoon in my Buick."

"All those afternoons you said you were going down to the Knights of Columbus to play cards," Mary said, shaking her head.

"Sorry, old girl, but it wouldn't do to tell you the truth." He looked at Hafner. "I knew by Tuesday what he was up to. I watched him case the school and the street where the little girl lived over in Dutchtown. But he didn't make a move, so I didn't either. Then I realized he was waiting for Wednesday. The twentieth anniversary of his last killing."

Spola drove in to Carson Avenue on Wednesday morning and staked out the church van. When Frawlic came for the van, the old detective knew he had his man.

"He had a kitten with him, Haffy. That was the bait." His voice, growing weaker, was barely above a whisper. "I followed him one more time over to Dutchtown, to Crossman Street. I parked around the corner and took a walk, just an old man shuffling down the sidewalk. I saw the little girl come up from the other way, and sure enough Frawlic hops out of the van with the kitten and opens up the side door. That's when I came up behind him and stuck my old Police Special, my S&W .38, behind his ear."

Mary Spola gasped, then lowered her face into her hands. Father Joe and Sister Matty looked nearly as dismayed, although perhaps for mixed reasons. To have had a sick killer in their midst, preying on little girls . . .

"I think that's all I'm gonna tell you, boys," Spola said hoarsely, watching his wife. "Except that you needn't bother searching the house for my gun. It's in a watery grave somewhere."

Hafner drew himself up and tapped his pen against the notepad. "You could've called us in, or made a citizen's arrest on the spot, Tony."

"Yep, I could have. But I kept thinkin', what happens if I call the cops in and Frawlic gets nailed for stalking the girl? So maybe he goes back to prison for a few more years. The son of a bitch is only forty-one. He gets out again, he's still got time to do a lot of damage. Me, on the other hand . . ."

"That's when you decided it was worth trading what's left of your life for the killer's?"

"I decided a long time ago that was a fair trade. No, what took awhile was deciding if it was worth trading my soul." He glanced at Father Joe, and what passed for a smile formed on his lips. "Me and Ben Garfield talked about it, ya know, like everything else. I can remember I says to him once, 'So Ben, what d'ya think? If I had the guy dead to rights—I'm sayin' I knew, okay? And instead of bringing him in, risking him getting off or maybe copping a plea and getting out in ten years, I just put him down like a sick animal. One to the back of the head. Now, you think God'd hold it against me? Condemn me to hard time?' And you know what Ben said?"

"What'd he say?"

"He gave that little shrug of his and he says, 'Ah—maybe a cup of coffee in purgatory. You spend a little time, say a few prayers, and it's straight on up with the angels.'" Spola sighed wistfully. "I hope he was right."

"Yeah," Hafner said solemnly. "I hope so too, Tony."

And Father Joe added, "Amen."

Epilogue

The old cop knew what he was talking about.

The DA's office spent weeks reviewing the evidence that Hafner and Greene laid out for them on the Frawlic case. They were still dithering, trying to decide whether to seek an indictment, when Tony Spola died. His heart gave out one November afternoon near Thanksgiving. He was sitting out in the breezeway when it happened, bundled up, smoking a cigarette.

Harold Hafner was one of his pallbearers. At the service, one of Tony's—and Hafner's—favorite songs was played. Sinatra, of course. "My Way."

The *Times-Democrat* ran a story under the byline of L.J. Trudeau, exposing Jeffrey Frawlic as the alphabet killer. It had all of the facts except the who and the why behind Frawlic's own murder. Lena had her suspicions but no hard proof. And no matter how many dinners she offered him, Kelvin Greene refused to tell her a thing.